the
salt
messages

the salt messages

RICK STRATER

LANIER
PRESS

LANIER PRESS *an imprint of BookLogix*

Alpharetta, GA

Copyright © 2020 by StraterEdge Publishing, LLC

ISBN: 978-1-63183-915-3 - Paperback
ISBN: 978-1-63183-916-0 - Hardcover
eISBN: 978-1-63183-917-7 - ePub
eISBN: 978-1-63183-918-4 - mobi

Printed in the United States of America   1 0 2 9 2 0

♾This paper meets the requirements of ANSI/NISO Z39.48-1992 (Permanence of Paper)

Erin, you inspired me to ask the questions I was afraid to ask, to listen, and to try to learn. I love you.

Brad, thank you for meeting with me and shepherding me through my journey. Your patience with my unending questions is amazing and a blessing.

Human beings, all over the earth, have this curious idea that they ought to behave in a certain way. . . . Consequently, this Rule of Right and Wrong . . . must somehow or other be a real thing—a thing that is really there, not made up by ourselves. . . .

We want to know whether the universe simply happens to be what it is for no reason or whether there is a power behind it that makes it what it is. . . .

The only way in which we could expect [that power] to show itself would be inside ourselves as an influence or a command trying to get us to behave in a certain way.

—C. S. Lewis, *Mere Christianity*

A new commandment I give to you, that you love one another as I have loved you.

—John 13:34

PROLOGUE

I can't believe I'm writing this. My hands are shaking so much I can barely type. I keep hitting the wrong keys. I argued with myself at length about whether to share the events of the last few weeks with *anyone*, and I'm not sure if it was the angel on my left shoulder or the devil on my right who won the debate. Well, probably not a devil, if all this actually happened. But, as much as it scares me, I'm writing this because I'm pretty sure that's what I'm *supposed* to do. That's why I think I was given a seat at the table.

When people read this, some are going to say I'm absolutely bonkers and dismiss me as "just another nutcase." Others are going to call me a heretic and want to drive a wooden stake through my heart. Then, there are the wacky types who are going to want to touch me and follow me around burning incense and hoping to share my every experience. I would probably fall into the first group, because I have to admit, my story sounds like someone who has had a psychotic break. Still, I'm not sure I could find fault with any of those reactions.

I swear that everything I write here is true to the best of my knowledge and that these things took place exactly as I have captured them. I didn't make notes at first, but the deeper I got into all of this, the more I knew I needed to make a daily accounting in order to try to not miss anything important. So, I'm sharing what is essentially my diary of what happened.

When I reviewed my notes and imagined myself in the role of a third party reading them, I occasionally found that I needed to add commentary for clarity. Where I have done that, I have tried to make it obvious. But, I did not go back and change the original content.

As background, I think it is also important to note that I don't take drugs. Never have. I drink alcohol, but for the last fifteen years, I've been doing a cleanse between New Year's and Valentine's Day. I did so again this year. Since the events I am sharing took place during this time, I was not under the influence of alcohol. Nevertheless, I readily admit that while all this was taking place, I thought seriously about having a drink . . . no, drinks.

Let's call me Tom. That's not my name, but I need to try to protect me and my family from the consequences of writing about what happened. In a way, I suppose that by hiding behind a pseudonym, I'm as guilty as those who have denied things like this in the past, but I'm doing the best I can. I want you to know everything so you can decide for yourself if I'm certifiable, or if something beyond our normal sense of reality actually occurred.

In the end, it doesn't matter what you think of me. It's the story itself that I'm convinced is important, because it may very well matter what *you* decide to do with what I have to tell you.

THE LAST NORMAL DAY

My wife, Carol, and I live in a small town in Georgia.

Not surprisingly, Carol is not my wife's name. Like for me, and everyone else I reference in these notes, I have created fictitious names to try to keep each of us from the spotlight of public scrutiny while still allowing me to tell my story in as much detail as possible.

Life here is slow. Not glacial, but slow enough for people to know each other. We ask about our neighbors' families and take the time to actually listen to the answers. If someone has a problem, people genuinely want to know what they can do to help. When Jess C. Scott wrote that "friends are the family we choose," she captured the feel of our community.

We stumbled on this place six years ago when we were trying to escape the high taxes and cold weather of the Chicago suburbs. I wanted to live on the ocean. Carol wanted to live on a lake. We "compromised." We live on a lake. Carol is happy, so I am happy. Maybe I'll get an ocean in my next life . . .

In hindsight, Carol was probably right. The life we have here is idyllic. We have four seasons (a must for Carol): the summers are hot and humid, like in Chicago, but spring comes early, fall lasts into November, and winters are typically mild. Even when we have a cold snap, it rarely lasts longer than a couple of weeks or so before the midday thermometer again reaches fifty-plus.

The lake we live on is magnificently framed by mountains as a backdrop, and the golf course that's in our neighborhood is beautiful—too hard, but beautiful.

It is unusual for more than a few days to go by before one of our close neighbors decides to invite everyone to have cocktails. When I say "everyone," I mean about ten households around us. Most of the year, I love it. My annual cleanse is boring.

I originally started this habit of abstention for two reasons. I wanted to shed the extra pounds I add each holiday season, and I wanted to prove to myself that I could actually go six weeks without drinking. If it ever truly bothered me, I figured I would know I had a problem. So far, so good. Boring, but good.

There are roughly three hundred homes where we live, so it isn't surprising that there are many similar, tightly bonded cliques in the neighborhood. Carol is the definition of an extrovert. I'm certain there's a picture of her in the dictionary when you look it up. So, we are somewhat amorphous and float with ease among several groups. In most, I am readily recognized as "Carol's husband." Our close neighbors actually know my name, but I am under no delusions. I'm still Carol's husband.

Don't get me wrong, I'm okay with that. I'm happy she takes point. The booze, appetizers, and chitchat are good at any of the get-togethers. The people are warm and very engaging. The banter is sometimes sharp, but always in good humor.

Until the last few days, I didn't think much of how we happened to find this place. To me, it was a lucky coincidence. Now, I remember someone once telling me there are no coincidences.

Carol and I were putting up Christmas decorations right after Thanksgiving. When it comes to Christmas, Carol is like George Patton. She has a plan and that plan is going to be executed—period. I take orders like a buck private. When we were young and newly married, I made the occasional mistake of having opinions about Christmas. With age and experience come wisdom. Now I almost always swallow those ideas because I learned Carol's ideas are actually much better than mine, anyway, and I don't like the idea of throwing myself in front of a juggernaut.

While we were decorating the front-porch railing with the obligatory garland, I noticed one of the stones had come off the chimney.

Our home is cedar shake shingled with a cedar roof. The foundation and chimney are stone. Well, I didn't look closely enough when we bought the house. There is stone, then there is stone. Our variety is what one contractor I hired to do some remodeling called "lick and stick." It's concrete that is shaped and colored to look like stone. You know, like the stuff they use at theme parks. When it's put up right, it looks real enough. But, as it ages, the color fades and the edges start to show. I could use those same words to describe me, so I'm not being critical, merely making an observation.

We have a guy, John, who does work for us on the house. He's a genius when it comes to stonework. Last summer we reconstructed the detached garage and converted it into a carriage house. I had wanted to use natural stone on the foundation, but Carol quickly nixed that. Not only would it have been way too expensive, it would have made me want to change the rest of the house to match. That was totally out of the budget.

John's stonework on the foundation of the garage made the rest of the faux stone on the house look shabby in comparison. I floated the idea of at least having John change it on the house, but that was shot down too. Carol was absolutely right. We couldn't afford it, even though it would have looked much better.

Still, we needed John to replace the piece that had come off the front of the chimney. There had been a fairly significant windstorm a couple of nights earlier. It probably had dislodged itself then.

Both Carol and I looked for the missing piece of stone, but couldn't find it. I sent John a text and explained what we needed and asked if he had any left over from doing the garage. John sent me a note back telling me he would be over in a couple of days.

When John came by, he said he didn't have any extra stone and asked if I had anything from what we had originally taken off the garage. I told him there were only a few and showed him what I had. Nothing fit. He looked back over the area Carol and I had previously searched and happened to find the missing stone in a small tree next to the chimney.

I told John that Carol and I had looked at that tree, as well as around and under the surrounding shrubs, but hadn't seen it. Secretly, I was thankful Carol hadn't been able to find it, either. She is always (correctly) telling me I usually don't look carefully enough for something before deciding it isn't there. I'm not sure if she's right because of a genetic flaw that keeps men from finding things that are right in front of us or if ADD simply kicks in when I have to search for something I'm not that committed to finding. Either way, John found the stone Carol and I had both missed.

John figured he needed a thirty-foot ladder to do the job. He didn't have one but said he could borrow it, and he promised to be back in a few days.

Those few days turned into a few weeks. I heard John had hurt his back and wasn't working, plus it was the holidays, so I didn't bug him about it.

I was reading in the kitchen midday on January 8 when I heard a hollow metallic sound outside the house. I finally recognized it as an aluminum ladder being hoisted into position and went to the front door to find John, with the missing stone in hand already loaded with concrete mud to replace it on the chimney.

Without a doubt, that was the last normal thing that happened to me until—well, I don't want to get ahead of myself.

WEDNESDAY, JANUARY 8

I greeted John with a smile. "Happy New Year!" I asked him about his back. He said he wasn't sure what had happened. He had tried to sit up in bed one day a week before Christmas and his back had just locked up. It had gotten better after a few days, but he had coincidentally developed a sinus infection.

He went to see his doctor, but the she wouldn't give him anything for it because he didn't have a temp. A week later, after the sinus infection had developed into something major that caused swelling in his face and even made his teeth hurt, the doc finally agreed to give him meds.

When I asked him how he was feeling now, John said he was better. In addition to the medication, the doctor had given him a prescription to go to the salt spa next to the Piggly Wiggly in town. It was some place called Sea Breeze.

Everything about that sounded weird to me. Prescription to a salt spa? Who the hell does that? And why a salt spa—whatever that was?

He told me he had gone to the salt spa and thought it helped, but he said he had needed the medicine, anyway, and was much better now.

Then, John glanced at me uncomfortably before looking away. After a long pause, he took a deep breath that not only caused his chest to expand, but raised his shoulders. He audibly exhaled. It seemed to me he was someone struggling with something big, and he had finally summoned up the courage to deal with it.

John looked back at me and said, "You've always been good enough to listen to me and to give me advice."

I replied, "Sure, John. I appreciate all you do for us. You're not only someone who does work for us, you're a friend. What's on your mind?"

He nodded. "Can we talk for a few minutes?"

"Of course."

"I mean, can we go into the house and sit down for a few minutes?"

John never came into the house, even when I invited him, so I knew he wanted to talk about something important.

"Yeah, absolutely, John." I led the way into the house and suggested we go into the kitchen, motioning him to a spot on the cushioned, L-shaped bench that provided seating around two sides of the round breakfast table.

John ignored my suggestion and plopped down on a stool at the island, so I leaned against the counter opposite from where he was sitting.

"What it is, John? It's obvious that you're troubled about something. Is it the business?"

A year earlier, John had decided to go into business for himself. Before making that call, he had been working for someone else who kept screwing him. John was a gifted craftsman and put in long hours. He had wanted my opinion about whether it made sense for him to go out on his own.

John had given me an idea of what he was earning with the other guy. We did some quick, back-of-the-envelope calculations and figured out what he would need to keep himself whole. It looked like a no-brainer.

I had a couple of jobs that needed to be

done, and Carol was working on a project with the neighborhood I thought he could win if he bid for it aggressively. Neighbors across the street were planning on redoing their front sidewalk and driveway. He wouldn't be able to rely upon us long term, but with even these few jobs, he would earn roughly what he would make in five months with his current employer.

My only words of caution were that it would be important for him to continue to prospect while he was working. Word of mouth would help, but he would need to always be actively looking for the next project. And he would need to set aside enough money for the inevitable slow months during winter.

As far as I knew, it seemed everything with the business was going well. He was always busy.

John said, "No, the business is good. It

isn't that." After another long pause, he said, "You know me. I'm an honest guy. Did I ever tell you I was in the Navy?"

"No, I don't remember you ever sharing that with me. When was that?"

"About ten years ago, but that doesn't matter. What matters is that when I was in the Navy, I was a signalman. You know, we have all kinds of sophisticated ways to communicate between ships, but because there is always the risk that electronic communications could be jammed or down for some other reason, I had to learn semaphore as well as blinker communication. You know semaphore. It uses flags that each have a specific meaning. Blinker communication uses old-fashioned Morse code. Of course, messages can be encrypted, even when we're using Morse code. But, a signalman needs to be very good at sending and receiving. I was *very* good."

I wondered where the hell this was going,

but just said, "I'm sure you were. That's interesting. I never knew that."

John waved off my attempt at appearing genuinely rapt by his revelation. "I'm only telling you because of what happened last week."

"Okay. Sorry. What happened?"

Another big sigh. "Well, like I said, the doc sent me to the salt spa. I was really hurting, so I was ready to try anything. When I got there, they put me in this dark room, took away my cell phone, and made me take off my shoes. There was rock salt on the floor, several inches deep, and the walls were made to resemble what I imagine a salt mine would look like. They were bumpy and looked greyish-white, from what little I could see.

"No one else was in the room. In fact, the only things there besides the salt were six or seven zero-gravity chairs. Not sure why they called them that. Looked like lawn chairs to me. Music was playing softly. I'd never been to a spa before, but I'm betting it was spa music. The kind of music designed to put you to sleep.

"The person who led me into the room gave me a warm blanket, then told me to pick a chair and cover myself with the blanket. He said a sensor would measure the amount of salt in the air and add more as needed. The salt air is supposed to be good for breathing problems, like my sinus infection.

"I was hurting so much I would have stuck my tongue in a light socket if the doc had told me it would make me better. She sent me to this salt spa, so I was going to do whatever I was told to do.

"After I settled myself into the chair, I noticed there were hundreds of little white lights in the ceiling. You know, like Christmas-tree lights. They were blinking in a random pattern. I assumed they were just part of the plan to put me to sleep. In fact, the guy told me to relax and sleep if I wanted. He said he would be back in forty-five minutes. Then he left.

"I'll admit, it was relaxing. The music was soft and calming. There wasn't any other sound except an occasional hissing from a nozzle in one corner when salt mist was added. I'm not sure how long I was in there when I noticed it. Maybe twenty or thirty minutes."

John's discomfort had disappeared as he told his story, but now it resurfaced. Once again he stopped.

I prompted him, "When you noticed what?"

The words came out from him one at a time.

"A light . . . one to my left and down below my feet from where I was lying . . . seemed to get much brighter than the others. I couldn't help but notice it. It was sorta like it was demanding my attention. Then, instead of blinking randomly, I realized it was blinking out a message."

"A message?"

"Yes, in code. Like when I was in the Navy."

"Wow. Are you sure?"

"Yes. Remember, I was very good."

"I'm sure you were. Maybe you had fallen asleep."

"No, I pinched myself." John showed me his arm. "See, I drew blood."

Looking at the bruise, I said, "Ouch. That looks like it hurt."

"It did."

"So, maybe the guy who put you in the room was just messing with you."

"I thought about that, but how would he know I can read code?"

"Fair point."

"Besides, there is no way he could have sent me this message."

"Why?"

"Because the message was, 'Tell Tom and bring him here.' It wants to talk to you."

I like John, but his comment sounded like a load of BS. I'm not big on being played, and my curt, knee-jerk reaction was a bit more abrasive than it should have been. "What! Come on, John. This is a joke, right? Did Carol put you up to this? Am I being punked? Where's the camera?"

"I know this sounds crazy, Tom. That's what makes me so uncomfortable about coming to you with this. Like I said, I have always appreciated your advice. I don't want to say or do anything that would make you think less of me. But this thing actually happened, and whoever sent me that message wants to talk to you."

I shook my head. "You're either a really good actor, in which case you're wasting your talents and you should be on the stage, or you truly believe this. I just can't buy that some light, or whoever is controlling it, wants to talk to me. You admitted you were sick. Maybe you had a fever and you imagined all of this. At least something like that would make sense."

"I was sick and in pain, but I didn't have a fever. I hadn't taken any pain medication. I can't explain it, but it happened—for real."

"Okay, just for the sake of argument, let's say you genuinely did get a message and you're supposed to bring someone named Tom to the salt spa—to Sea Breeze—with you. Did it say it wanted to talk with Tom Adams who lives on Lakeside Drive?"

John looked at me with an expression that seemed somewhat desperate. "No, it simply said to bring Tom. But somehow I knew exactly who it wanted me to bring. You."

I stared at John for a few moments. As bizarre as his tale was, the sincerity in his voice and the passion in his delivery were compelling. He was leaning forward on his stool. Having decided to tell me his story, he was committed to getting my acceptance of what he was sharing.

At the time, I was less sympathetic of his need for me to believe him than I am now as I tell you what happened next.

"Okay, John. I absolutely believe that *you* believe what you just told me. What do you suggest we do?"

"Come to Sea Breeze with me. I'll schedule a time for us and I'll even pay for it. So, if nothing happens, you will have only wasted forty-five minutes."

"You're not simply trying to get me into a dark room so you can have your way with me, are you?"

John started to get upset and protest.

I raised my hand. "I'm kidding, John. I know this is important to you. I would be lying if I didn't tell you I think it all sounds weird, and it will look a little odd for me to be going to a salt spa with you—I'd better tell Carol I'm going and why—but I'll do it."

John looked relieved. "Great! I'll try to book us a time for tomorrow and let you know." I paid him for cementing the stone back onto the fireplace and he left.

About fifteen minutes later, he sent me a message telling me we had an appointment for the next morning at 10:30.

Carol had been with our oldest daughter, Liz, redecorating the bedroom for one of Liz's three girls. When she came home, I shared John's story with her. Unlike me, Carol is fairly spiritual and always ready to give someone the benefit of the doubt. She agreed it sounded strange, but she also thought it was a good idea for me to go and check it out.

The only thing I asked of her was to not tell

anyone about it until afterward. I still felt uncomfortable about what I had agreed to do, and I preferred to share it as a laugh after the fact, rather than have it hanging out there as a strange event with a yet unknown outcome.

Carol promised to not tell anyone and said she was excited to hear what happened.

THURSDAY, JANUARY 9

I was up during the night. The thought of going to this salt spa bothered me. It just seemed creepy. I've always been open to leading-edge ideas, especially ones that are disruptive. I like finding a better way to do things. But Carol can attest to the fact that I've also been closed to anything that strikes me as smarmy. A salt spa sounded too much like snake oil to me. I grabbed my phone, took it with me into the bathroom so I wouldn't bother Carol, and did some digging.

It turns out halotherapy isn't a new fad. It's

been around for a long time. *Halo* comes from the Greek word for salt. Apparently, healers have been recommending dry salt therapy for more than two thousand years—which may only prove that quackery isn't new.

We've all heard the beach air is therapeutic, but I have generally thought of that more in the context of enjoying the warmth of the sun on my skin, the calming effect of listening to the rhythm of the surf, and playing in the sand while smelling the ocean, as opposed to some kind of genuine health benefit from breathing salt air.

On the other hand, I've always kind of had a negative impression of salt mines. But, I read miners in Poland's salt mines have notably fewer respiratory ailments than the general population. Who knew? So, there may be some scientific evidence that adds a modicum of credence to the idea of dry salt therapy.

Proponents claim such therapy can lower inflammation in the lungs and even lessen the risks and severity of various respiratory maladies, such as asthma and allergies, sinus infections, and supposedly even chronic obstructive pulmonary disease (COPD). I also read it can improve blood sugar levels by impacting cellular activity. Salt is a natural disinfectant, as well.

The list of the benefits gets quite long, and therefore, from my cynical perspective, less credible. But, it seemed to me from a quick search there was at least enough substance to withhold final judgment for the moment.

Reading all this made me wonder about the phrase "salt of the earth," which various dictionaries say is a term of respect for someone trustworthy and honest. In Matthew 5:13, it seems Jesus said of his disciples that they were "the salt of the earth" because they were charged with spreading the messages of Christ.

I kept searching for more. Apparently, there are a lot of references to salt in the Bible. And it seems Roman soldiers were sometimes paid in salt. (I'd have preferred cash.)

So, there are all these positive references to salt. But if it's so great, why does it raise our blood pressure? And why was Lot's wife turned into a pillar of salt when she looked back on Sodom and Gomorrah? Talk about too much of a good thing . . .

Spice of life aside, I had no doubts about the flashing lights. There were only three options. One: John was making all this stuff up. Two: John had been ill or asleep and imagined everything. Three: Someone was messing with John. John had been too serious for me to believe he was setting me up for a joke.

Planning on going to the gym after I met John at Sea Breeze, I put on my workout clothes when I rolled out of bed a little before 8:00. It wasn't a cold morning, especially for January.

(Thank God we had moved to Georgia.) Still, I needed a jacket, so I pulled one over my head, grabbed my water bottle that I had primed with amino acids for my workout, and went out the door around 9:00 so I could go to Cuppa, our local coffee and tea joint, before my date with destiny. I needed a tea.

I drive a Jaguar F-type and I love to hear the engine start. The guy who sold it to me said something about ball bearings that keep the oil up in the pan so the car redlines when it starts. I don't know squat about cars, but that sounded reasonable to me. Regardless, my car roars when it starts, screams to sixty-plus, and is flat-ass sexy. The car constantly gets compliments. It also causes some people to act like buttheads.

This morning on my way to Cuppa, some douchebag kid in a piece of junk with the springs cut so it would ride lower to the ground pulled up beside me at a light.

Adam Sandler's "Ode to My Car" immediately popped into my thoughts and I couldn't get the song out of my head until my experience at the Sea Breeze.

This kid's exhaust had been modified, too, so it made a lot of noise. When the light changed, he got on it. I decided he wasn't worth it and passed on embarrassing him. Just as well. I saw the blue lights from a sheriff come to life as the kid sped by the side road where he had been sitting. Seeing this kid pull over brought a smile to my face.

Normally, I would have ordered ahead from Cuppa and taken my tea with me, but this morning I wanted to just sit and relax, catch up on the morning news, and try to get a sense of what the stock market was going to do for the day. Was I going to be happy or get hammered in the market—again? I had had more than my share of that last week. It would be good to have an up day. So, I went in and stood in line to place my order.

A woman so large I couldn't see the barista in front of her was in line ahead of me. She was intently asking about nearly every food item in the display case. Not only did she want to know about the calorie count (she should have thought about that before), she was asking whether they were spicy, which she didn't like, or too salty. As my blood pressure started to elevate, she vacillated about which was right for her. It was like watching one of the contestants on *Let's Make a Deal* argue with herself about which door to choose: "Two! No, one . . . three!" Then, once she finally made her food choice, she repeated the process with her drink order. The barista was patient. I wasn't. I'm sure the woman could sense my head turns and eye rolls, even though they were to her back.

When it was finally my turn, I made my

order in a flash to show how it should be done. As I stepped over to where customers wait for their completed orders, the woman looked at me and smiled. "I'm sorry I took so long."

I gave her an unctuous smile in return and said with an easily discernible note of self-righteous indignation, "There are a lot of choices."

My order was ready, but I had missed the opening bell of the market and my stocks were once more down. The prospects for the morning were pointing down, as well, on a number of levels.

I arrived at Sea Breeze about fifteen minutes early. John had explained that I needed to complete some paperwork before our session, since I had never been there before.

Walking into the spa, on shelves right inside the door, I noticed an array of glowing lamps I assumed were supposed to look like large salt crystals. Lit from within, they all emitted a warm glow. They were obviously for sale. I didn't see price tags, but I was guessing they weren't cheap. If only they played some cheesy spa music . . .

The wood parquet floor was covered with plush oriental rugs. Several chairs had been carefully clustered around the reception area. They looked comfortable, but by design not so comfortable that acolytes of salt therapy would be happy just to wait there. This was simply the anteroom.

Barry, the owner/manager of the Sea Breeze, greeted me in nasally tones and I introduced myself. He was excited to meet me as a first-timer and, with flair, handed me a clipboard and pen to get started.

I remember Barry from when I was a teenager. Well, not Barry, but people like Barry. Barry was an *Oh wow*.

I was a teenager in the '60s. Carol and I have four kids who always assumed that because of when I grew up, I smoked weed, or worse. No amount of explaining that I didn't had ever convinced them otherwise. I've never understood that, since they all admit I'm a straight arrow on everything else. They (rightfully) consider my integrity beyond reproach. Why would I lie?

In their defense, I'm certain I didn't do my case much good when I revealed I knew how to roll a cigarette. My high school buddy, Dave, and I had bought loose-leaf tobacco and rolling paper and practiced until we were experts at it. We pretended the taste was great, and with absolutely zero evidence to support us, convinced ourselves the leaf we were using had less harmful chemicals than cigarettes made by the big tobacco companies. In reality, we just wanted to be cowboys. Well, cowboys without the dust, hard work, saddle sores, and sleeping on the ground. You know, cowboys like those on TV and the movies.

No, I took a total of about three hits from a joint growing up and acknowledged that to my unbelieving kids, but I didn't like it and I didn't want to get in trouble.

On the other hand, an *Oh wow* was defined as one of those I had met in my teen years who was habitually attached to a bong or other delivery system, constantly stoned (like my roommate in college), and always saying things like: "That's heavy, man." "Like, man, this is some really good shit." "Out of sight." And, for some reason, it was imperative that each such statement was delivered in extremely nasally tones.

Yup, Barry was an *Oh wow*. Though I'm not sure from a business standpoint that it is advisable for someone promoting dry salt therapy to speak nasally.

The questions on the forms attached to the clipboard were slightly irritating. They asked about health issues with check boxes for Yes/No responses. But, it was obvious the questions were really there so *Oh wow* could upsell his services. They also captured my mobile number and email address so they could further clutter up my text and email with unwanted marketing junk. What I can't figure out is why whenever I'm asked for this kind of information, I don't just make up something.

I answered everything quickly, signed the papers in the appropriate places, then returned my clipboard and completed forms to *Oh wow* before plopping down in one of the reception chairs.

Fortunately, John came in almost as soon as my backside hit the seat. Because he was a returning customer, he didn't have to fill out forms or answer questions. We were simply shown back to the "salt cave."

There were about ten chairs scattered around the room, but no one other than John and I was booked for a session. The idea that John and I were going to be doing this by ourselves felt even weirder—if that was at all possible. When *Oh wow* gave me my warm blankie, I asked him if the salt was going to stick to my socks. He assured me it would not and walked into the room himself to prove it.

John took a chair and immediately stared at the ceiling. I assumed it was the seat he had been in the last time he was there. I sat several chairs away from him and mumbled to *Oh wow* something about John telling me the therapy was particularly helpful before faking a cough for good measure.

That elicited an enthusiastic response. *Oh wow* droned on about how the salt was going to help me, but I wasn't listening.

As soon as John and I were alone, I asked him when we should expect a transmission. He looked stung by my flippancy and pointed out the bulb I should be watching.

I didn't want to hurt his feelings, so I made an excuse and told him I was a little nervous about what was going to happen next. Probably at least partially true. His head bobbed in response. Then, we settled in and waited in silence.

After about fifteen minutes, just as I was drifting into a light slumber, John whispered loudly, "There! Do you see it? It's getting brighter and the others are dimming." He was pointing to the bulb he had told me to watch.

"I guess so. It's kinda hard to tell," I lied. It was clearly brighter than the other bulbs in the ceiling, but I wasn't ready to admit it. The bulb started blinking in some kind of pattern. I can't read Morse code, other than SOS, but it looked to me like it was sending out some kind of a message.

John said, "It thanked me for bringing you here. It also said I'm a good stonemason and a good person. It's proud of me for helping Mrs. Rodgers. She's a lady who recently had to put her husband into a nursing facility because he has Alzheimer's.

"She needed a project done that she couldn't afford. I told her I had found a quarry with an overage in the stone she wanted to use and I was able to get it really cheaply. Wasn't true, but she wouldn't have liked it if she knew I wasn't charging her what she thought was a fair price. Just a chance for me to give back."

"That's a nice story," I said, "but how do I know what it's saying? All I see is a blinking light."

"Well, you know 'cause I told you. But, the light also said it would take it from here."

"What the hell does that mean? And how would anyone know about this Mrs. Rodgers, unless you told someone?"

"Don't know."

I looked back at the flashing bulb. It was all gibberish to me. This was nuts. I started to throw off my blanket when I was stunned to suddenly realize I *could* read the code being flashed to me. It said, "Hi, Tom. Thanks for coming."

I turned to John. "Did you see that?"

"See what?"

"The bulb said 'hi' to me and thanked me for coming."

"What bulb?"

I was ready to give him hell for what I was now sure was a scam I had finally bought, but was stopped by a voice.

"John isn't kidding. He can't see the bulb any longer, nor can he hear me. He did what I asked him to do by convincing you to come meet with me. We don't need the flashing bulb, or Morse code, any longer. Let's just talk. Okay?"

"Who the hell is this? We're way too early for April Fool's. Did Carol put you up to this? Or is this Barry?"

"No. No, Tom. You know I'm not Barry,

and you also know neither John nor Carol is playing a trick on you."

I jumped up from my chair. "Okay, so I'll ask again. Who are you?"

"You already know the answer to that question too. You've been asking it for several months since your daughter was diagnosed with cancer. So, here I am. Let's talk."

"This is bull! Don't bring Reagan into this." As I bounded for the door, I looked at John, who seemed comatose and oblivious to what was happening. To the ceiling, I said, "I'm done with this game, whoever you are."

I grabbed the doorknob and turned it, but it just spun in circles. I started banging on the door and shouting for Barry. "Hey, let me out of here!"

"I'm afraid Barry—you call him *Oh wow*, don't you—can't hear you. Why not take a seat and let's talk for a few minutes? Then, you can decide if we should talk again or not. Entirely up to you. What do you say?"

I was pissed. I don't like it when I'm not in control or unable to figure out something. This situation hit both buttons at the same time. I reacted by stomping around the room and hyperventilating.

The voice said, "I know you're angry, Tom. You're angry about what Reagan has been going through. You're angry about a lot of things you can't control.

"Do you know you acted the same way when you were told you couldn't start first grade because your birthday missed the school's cutoff? You also did so when your parents moved you the next year after you had completed the first semester of first grade and the new school didn't offer half-grades. Your parents decided to put you in first grade again instead of second. Remember?"

"Of course I remember, but how the hell do you know about that?"

The voice laughed. "I know quite a lot

about you. I also know you felt self-conscious about being older than other kids in your grade. You didn't want anyone to think you were 'dumb' and that you had flunked a grade. But, if your first school hadn't had a cutoff and half-grades, and if your parents hadn't decided to have you put into a first-grade class in your next school, you would have graduated high school before Carol got there as a sophomore and you wouldn't have met the love of your life. There really are no coincidences, are there, Tom?"

I stopped stomping and gaped slack-jawed at the again randomly blinking lights. Groping for the closest chair, I fell down into it and asked, "Who *are* you?"

"I'm someone who loves you, and I want us to get to know each other better. Just like you do."

"Is this for real, or am I having some kind of hallucination?"

"Nope, you're fine. This is absolutely real."

"Why are we talking in a salt spa?"

"Why not? John had a sinus infection. His doctor recommended a treatment here. He has special skills reading Morse code. You know him. He knows you. It's quiet here and the music isn't bad. But, we can do this somewhere else if you would rather."

I was dumbfounded. "I guess this is as good a place as any. Are you sure I'm not being set up? God, I hate being wrong and stupid."

"I know."

"Why can't I see you?"

"Let's take this one step at a time. Same time tomorrow? Barry's calendar is open for the next week or so at 10:30."

"Why? Why do you want to talk to me?"

"The invitation has always been there. But you only accepted it a couple of months ago when you started meeting with Pastor Bill to discuss the books he recommended to help you with your journey. You were particularly taken with C. S. Lewis's argument in *Mere Christianity* that we all have an inner voice that knows the difference between right and wrong, and that inner voice is a clear clue God exists in everyone. I like that book too.

"He opened your eyes and your heart to a new conversation. I know you pushed back on some of Lewis's ideas and those presented by others. Good for you. I'm not agreeing or disagreeing with you, but good for you. I want you to think and challenge the thinking of others."

"So, we're going to . . . talk? Just 'the Great Oz' and me. Really?"

The disembodied voice chuckled. "Funny. I've never been called 'the Great Oz' before. You are reasonably quick, Tom. I like that. You want to talk, don't you?"

I let "reasonably" pass without comment. "Yes. No. People will think I'm crazy. Carol will think I'm crazy. *I* think I'm crazy. I'm talking with a voice in a salt cave because John here was getting messages from the beyond. I think that's one of the definitions of crazy."

"I know. That's a big risk. It has been since I started talking with people a long time ago. But, you'll have to decide whether it's worth taking that risk. Totally your call."

While I sat there thinking, I was digging my nails into my hands until I heard, "Does that help?"

"What?"

"Hurting yourself."

"Oh. No, I suppose it doesn't. Okay, I feel sort of stupid, but I'll be here tomorrow."

"Great."

That was it. I heard a ding that sounded like a timer chiming and *Oh wow*, er, Barry, came in to tell John and me our time was up, then left to let us gather our shoes.

I looked at John and asked him how he liked the session. He told me he had fallen asleep shortly after getting there and it had been very relaxing. When I asked him if he noticed anything strange, he looked at me blankly and shook his head. Then, he snapped his fingers. "You changed chairs, didn't you? Why?"

I told him I had because I was bothered by a light from the corner of the room. No big deal.

Then it dawned on me. There *was* a light in the corner. I was pretty sure the room was monitored by a camera, and perhaps there was a mic, as well.

I grabbed my shoes without putting them on and hurried out to Barry.

"Hey, Barry. I'm guessing that you have a camera and a mic in that room for security purposes."

Barry looked uncomfortable. "I do, and we record each session in case anyone has a problem. Why, was there a problem?"

"No, none at all. I just wanted to see whether I actually fell asleep or if I was awake the entire time. I also heard a noise at one point. Maybe it was John snoring. I know he slept. It would help if I could see the recording of our session."

"That's against our policy."

"Why? You're the owner, aren't you?"

"Well, yeah."

"What's the purpose of recording each of these sessions?"

"As I said, I have them in case there is a problem. Once a session ends, I have each person who has a treatment sign a form asking if everything was satisfactory and providing details if there was an issue of any kind. If there weren't any issues, the recordings are deleted. If anyone has a concern, I have video proof of what took place."

"Good thinking. So, just let me watch our session. You can watch it with me. I want to see if I fell asleep. My wife has been telling me I have sleep apnea. I feel great, by the way, and I want to book another session for tomorrow at the same time as today. Anyway, if I did fall asleep and didn't have breathing issues, I can tell her it is probably because of your therapy."

Barry was a little more receptive. "I'm so glad you enjoyed it." Turning to John, he asked, "Will you be coming tomorrow too?"

John replied, "No, I told Tom about Sea Breeze and he asked me to come with him today because he had never been here and he has had problems with his sinuses too. But, I've got too much to do. Y'all are on your own."

I tried not to react to John's explanation, but if anyone had been watching me closely, they would have been able to tell my poker face wasn't going to win many hands.

I said to John, "I know you've got things to do this afternoon. Thanks for introducing me to Sea Breeze." I turned back to Barry and asked again about watching our session. He made sure John didn't mind and agreed when John gave his blessing.

The camera and the mic showed nothing. What a surprise. The only thing I saw was I got up out of my chair in the middle of the session and sat in another without walking to the door. I just sat in the second chair and covered myself with my blanket. But, my back was to the camera at that point. I couldn't see my face, so I don't know if my eyes were closed.

I may be absolutely nuts. I simply don't understand how what I *remember* happening could have. There is no corroborating evidence to support it. John has a very different recollection about why we came here today than I do. He didn't hear or remember what I did—including the light flashing out a message in code. And, Barry's camera and mic picked up zip. It *couldn't* have happened. I'm going to go back tomorrow to prove I dreamed it or something.

When I got home, Carol asked me how my session went and whether I thought it helped my sinuses. That completely blew me away. Her question suggested that, like John, she believed I was going to Sea Breeze because of an issue I had, rather than John's revelation that blinking lights had sent him a message asking him to bring me with him to the spa.

I started to ask her why in the world she was pretending we hadn't had a very different conversation yesterday, but in the end, decided to leave it alone. If for some reason she didn't remember what we had talked about and her promise to not tell anyone until I came home, I wasn't ready to have a discussion that would make me sound like a mental case. I'm sure I fell asleep. Maybe I actually did have a sinus problem and dreamt the rest . . . but it seemed so *real*.

I made the decision to take notes about my trip to Sea Breeze and record them each time I visit. So, I summarized the events of January 8 and 9 here to the best of my recollection. I am certain I haven't captured each word of dialogue perfectly, but these notes are correct to the best of my ability. Some of the notes above may appear extraneous. They're not. I added them because of what took place over the next several days.

FRIDAY, JANUARY 10

I went to the gym before the spa today. I wanted to make sure I was fully alert. Doing a workout is exhausting and invigorating at the same time. There is very little chance of me falling asleep after a ninety-minute workout.

Barry didn't seem to mind that I was a little sweaty when I arrived. I hadn't thought about the fact that I would be sitting in his chairs. I apologized, but he told me he disinfects each chair after a guest leaves and pointed out that the salt air is a natural disinfectant anyway (as I had already read). He said my exercise would have opened my airways, allowing me to better take in the salt air. So, no harm done.

I'm not sure if anxious or nervous or foolish best describes my feelings as Barry got me settled. Maybe all three.

The door to the room clicked shut and I slid under the warm blanket. It was a good thing the room was cool, because I was still a little warm from my workout, so the blanket came down quickly.

I waited. As I did, I was surprised when I started to shiver. Afterward, I realized nerves were causing me to chill, making me again cover myself with the blanket. I often react that way when I am especially anxious about something. If nothing happened, it would be easy to chalk the events of the last two days as a dream and perhaps an overly active imagination. But if something did . . .

My internal clock told me I was nearing the end of my session. Nothing had happened and

I started to laugh at myself. Then, I heard the same voice I remembered. "Hi, Tom. I wanted to give you some time to relax and think before we continued our conversation. Hope you had a good workout. You ready to talk?"

"Oh. Sure, I guess so. I almost had myself convinced this whole thing never happened."

"I can understand that."

"We never established who you are."

"Well, we did. I told you I am someone who loves you."

"Someone who loves me? You mean like a dead relative or Santa Claus?"

"Interesting choices. Why dead relative?"

"I don't think anyone who is close to me and living would pull a stunt like this on me. I'm not sure they even could. I mean, this is a fairly intricate ruse."

"Reasonable thinking, but not a ruse. I'm glad to hear you still believe in Santa. So do I."

I qualified my comment. "You know what I

mean. Santa is magical. Every year I get caught up in movies about Christmas and have goosebumps as Santa's spirit seems to pervade, despite the hustle and bustle of buying presents and fighting crowded stores. I'd like to think I'm on Santa's Nice List."

"Most of the time you are. But, you know when you're doing things that put an asterisk after your name: 'mostly good.' And, you know Santa is watching you all year, not only at Christmas, don't you?

"You weren't exactly full of grace when you took pleasure in that young man getting a ticket yesterday morning. And what about the woman in line in front of you at Cuppa? You were all kindness, weren't you? It's only been two weeks since Christmas. The spirit of the holidays didn't last long, did it?"

I stammered, "How can you possibly know about those two?"

"Well, I'm a dead relative or Santa or

something. So, of course I know about them. What you don't know is that boy, Andy, has never had a parent who loves him. His father abandoned his mother when she got pregnant at eighteen. She was in and out of rehab for drug addiction before the county took her then three-year-old son away from her. Andy was shuttled from one foster care home to another growing up. He's a work in progress, but he is holding down a job and going to school. He wants to be a veterinarian, if he can get through his studies, because the only constant love he has known is a mutt he named Rocky. He had Rocky for almost eight years before he died. Andy thinks if he had known what to do for Rocky, he would have lived much longer.

"Andy bought his . . . what did you call it? Oh yeah, 'piece of junk' car himself, using money he made mowing lawns and doing odd jobs for neighbors. The car now lets him get to and from school and he works part time at a fast food restaurant. He thinks the car looks good with the springs cut, but he likes yours much better.

"The ticket he got won't break him. Even so, a fine of one hundred and fifty dollars represents almost a full week of his net pay. Still want to smile at him getting pulled over?"

My face burned with embarrassment.

"And, how about Sally at Cuppa? That's her name—the woman who was in front of you. You wouldn't have been pissy if it had been Salma Hayek in front of you, would you? I'm certain you would have offered to go over each menu item with her and even buy her whatever she chose, only to be sad and dejected when she walked out of the door and out of your life. But, you would have told that story every chance you got from that day forward."

My mouth hung open, but I didn't have a response.

"Did you think I don't know you find her beautiful? Of course she is. So is Sally.

Sally has fought her weight all her life and has tried every imaginable diet. Her doctors can't explain why she is so heavy. Nothing seems to be wrong with her that would prevent her from losing weight, but she can't lose it and keep it off.

"But, you should see her the way I see her. Her soul is so pure and bright that she shines from within. She also has the voice of an angel. When she sings, she can bring tears to your eyes. Yet no one would ever give her a part in musicals when she was in school because they could only see that she is heavy.

"The good news is that someone who heard Sally sing introduced her to a band that performs at her church. They love her. The congregation is closer to God when she performs. Sally also volunteers at the local children's hospital to take care of terminally ill children. They don't see her weight—they only feel the love in her embraces. When it is time for these children to come home, they all want their parents, they want their favorite stuffed animals, and every one of them wants Sally.

"I love you, but you know you can be a total ass sometimes, don't you? I think that's a technical term. It actually shows up on Santa's list next to your name: 'Mostly good, but can be an ass.'"

I started to cry.

"You know, you were given all the right stuff. You're tall and strong, and I suppose some might say good-looking. You could throw a fifty-yard pass on target when you were only fourteen. You loved baseball, but you quit playing. By the way, you had a wicked curveball. You're always beating yourself up for not doing anything with those gifts.

"You're smart too. You worked hard at school and kept going until you earned a graduate degree. You used that innate gift to have a successful career. Yet, you think you blew it when the boss asked you who should be president of your company and you didn't say, 'Me!' So, you think you failed. And how many times has someone asked you if you are in radio or TV because of your voice? You're afraid that when you get to the Pearly Gates and ask what you were supposed to do, St. Peter is going to say we kept trying to tell you.

"No, in your eyes, you haven't lived up to your potential and you feel guilty about it, don't you? Unfortunately, that guilt often colors how you treat others. It shouldn't. But, I want you to understand you are missing the point.

"Did you ever consider there was a *reason* why you didn't keep playing ball or step up and tell your boss you were ready for the job, or why you haven't done anything with your other talents? Maybe it is because you would have lost much more than you gained. Maybe it's because you would have been too impressed with yourself and would have made poor life decisions. Thank God you didn't do that.

"You have a love/hate relationship with yourself, don't you? Proud of yourself and at the same time embarrassed by the fact that you could have accomplished more with the gifts you were given. So, you sometimes make yourself feel better by finding fault with others, like Andy and Sally. Being proud of yourself isn't a sin. Well, it isn't unless you believe you alone deserve the credit for your accomplishments. Hint: You don't. But, self-flagellation isn't the answer, either."

I felt naked and ashamed.

"Yet, fear not. There's still hope for you. At least you stopped thinking of Barry as *Oh wow*.

Okay, I'm being tough on you. Don't get me wrong, you deserve it. But, I'm only talking about one side of you. Like everyone, you're much more than that.

"You are honest and faithful. Those are important foundations upon which to build your life and your relationships. It's because of your honesty and faithfulness that you are incensed by what you consider wrong. You don't like it when you think someone is being cheated or treated unfairly, and you aren't afraid of standing up and supporting that person when you see it happening. Unlike the way you reacted to Andy and Sally, you usually treat others with respect and kindness. People generally like you because of that. You have always given credit to your father for teaching you that everyone deserves respect. Respecting others was something *he* did very well."

I winced at the left-handed compliment.

"You have strong opinions, but you aren't

afraid to listen to others, and you are usually ready to admit it when you are wrong. (Carol may not necessarily agree with that comment, but it is generally true.)"

The voice commanded, "Tom, listen to me. You're an unfinished project, as every human is. There was a good reason ancient Greek authors wrote about tragic heroes. All of humanity is flawed. That's not a 'get out of jail free' card, it's just a fact. All people make mistakes. Making mistakes is part of the plan because it is what a person does after he or she errs that's important."

I could taste the salt in the tears running down my cheeks and into the corners of my mouth.

"That's enough for today. Let's get together again on Monday morning. But, I have an assignment for you between now and then."

I asked, "An assignment?"

"Yup. Between now and then, every time

you start to judge someone, I want you to stop and think about why the other person may have done whatever is bothering you. Then, I want you to try to remember it isn't your job to judge that person. We'll talk more about that next week."

I nodded weakly, then asked with more awareness, "Will I be able to see you next time?"

"When you're ready."

"What does that mean?"

"It means what it sounds like. When you're ready, you will see me."

Barry opened the door. My time was up. I thanked him and scheduled another session for Monday.

Leaving the spa, I sat in my car for a few minutes and wondered if maybe I was simply imagining the voice, or if someone or thing was actually trying to connect with me. The latter was too fantastic to be true. I really didn't believe it. So, why had I scheduled another appointment for Monday?

I laughed to myself and said out loud to no one, "Okay, see you Monday."

SATURDAY, JANUARY 11

Today was quiet and uneventful. Thank God. I needed it to be that way.

Carol asked me if I wanted to get into the hot tub. We did. The morning was bright and clear. There was a decided chill in the air, but the breeze was light, so the hot tub felt great.

Our hot tub talks are often accompanied by a bottle of champagne, just not during my cleanse. I asked Carol if she wanted any, but she said she didn't. I don't mean to make my annual abstention a burden on her or anyone else. It doesn't bother me if she has a drink or glass of wine, but she tries to be supportive. That's only one of the thousands of things I love about her.

I wanted to tell her about my visits to the salt spa and what had been happening, but I sensed that because she hadn't remembered me originally telling her about John and why I had agreed to go, it wouldn't be a good idea to broach the subject here. There must be a reason why she didn't remember.

One possibility is that I am absolutely crazy. Maybe, but I don't think so. Why would I suddenly go bonkers, unless maybe I have a brain tumor or something? Maybe I should get a scan. I'll hold off on that for now, but it may be a good idea if this thing continues. Making these notes is a good idea. If it is an illness, I may forget as it gets worse. The notes could help me or help Carol get me the right treatment.

If I'm dreaming all of it, surely I'll snap out

of this delusion. If it's a dream, it's elaborate, long, and involved. I wonder if I'll actually remember all of it? Anyway, a dream is another possibility. But, as long as I have my notes . . . Well, that assumes I *do* have my notes and I'm not just imagining I do.

I'm sure there are a number of plausible reasons I think this is all happening. The only one that doesn't make any sense whatsoever to me is that it is real. And, whoever is talking with me doesn't want Carol or anyone else to know, yet.

No, I opted to have a nice morning with Carol and not talk about the Sea Breeze.

We went to the movies in the afternoon, had an early dinner, and decided to play a game on my laptop.

It was a nice day. If it weren't for what was happening at the salt spa, I would call it normal.

SUNDAY, JANUARY 12

Carol and I went to church. When we're in town, we make it two or three times a month. I have to admit she had to drag me to services in the past, but since we moved to Georgia and started attending our church, I have been more engaged. The lead pastor is good. His messages speak to me.

Interestingly, his sermon this morning was focused on Christ telling his disciples he had a new commandment for them. He told them he wanted them to love each other as he had loved them, and to spread that message of love throughout the world. Considering my experiences at Sea Breeze and my discussions with the real or imaginary voice, I couldn't help but believe the message was targeted at me.

The congregation at our church is huge. On any given Sunday, there are at least two to three thousand people in attendance.

After the service, I felt a glow as I waited patiently for others to let them go ahead of me as we were all trying to leave.

The parking lot was, as always, a jumbled mess, despite the best efforts of the volunteers who try to get us out in an orderly fashion. But, again, I waited patiently for everyone to queue up to exit the church's lots. That is, I did until some asshole jumped into his truck and cut into line, blocking me and several others who had been waiting our turns. My glow completely faded.

This guy was wrong. It pissed me off. I

banged my left hand on the steering wheel and flailed my right hand in his direction saying to Carol, "What a jackass! We've all been here for almost a half an hour trying to get out and this guy comes bolting out of church, gets into his truck, and has the stones to get in front of the rest of us. That's so rude."

Carol looked at me and commented dryly, "You didn't listen very well to the message today, did you?"

"Yes, I did," I protested. "But this guy sure didn't."

"Maybe he has an emergency. Maybe one of his kids is hurt. You don't know what he's dealing with."

Carol is almost always giving someone the benefit of the doubt. It's endearing at one level, but it also sets her up to be taken advantage of. I knew I should have let it go, but I heard myself say, "Maybe he is late to get home to watch the playoffs."

I inwardly winced and felt more than a little guilty as I said it because I remembered both the message from today and what I imagined the voice had said to me last Friday. Both Andy and Sally came back to me.

Carol put her hand on my arm. "We're not in a hurry. It's a nice day. Why don't you turn on the radio?"

I knew she was right and that I was acting like a cretin, as I too often do. All the same, I almost reluctantly felt the tension ease in my shoulders. Change is hard and I'm stubborn, which makes it even harder. I finally smiled at Carol and turned on a jazz station she likes.

The logjam ended fairly soon after that and we headed home. Secretly, I knew I had again been tested, and again had failed. I was sure I was another step closer to Santa's Naughty List.

MONDAY, JANUARY 13

No sooner had Barry closed the door and I had settled in under my warm blanket when a blast of freezing cold air hit me in the face and a bright light nearly blinded me. I shaded my eyes and squinted to try to see what was happening. The surrounding darkness fell away and I found myself in an empty, brilliant white expanse.

"What the hell?"

"No, definitely not Hell."

I turned toward the voice and saw Santa Claus, or someone dressed like the generally accepted image of Santa. He was standing in the doorway of a large log-and-stone, single-story home that I'm sure hadn't been there a moment before. The home had a double-door entry covered by a porch with a hip roof. There was a massive stone fireplace on the front of the house to the left of the front door. The roof was steep, presumably to allow it to withstand the weight of the deep snow that had collected on it. The smoke wafting out of the chimney had the inviting scent of applewood. "Santa" waved me into the house.

"Don't just stay out there and freeze. Come on inside."

I stood there agape, momentarily unable to move, with only my blanket around my shoulders as protection against the bitter cold.

The light inside the house was a warm yellow, instead of the stark white outside. It seemed to be reaching out to me and drawing me toward it. Numbly, I started forward. Santa stepped aside to let me enter, followed me into the home, and closed the door behind us.

"Let's sit in front of the fire." Santa motioned us toward two overstuffed chairs that were separated by a rustic wood table with a lamp on it and knickknacks that reminded me of Christmas.

The floors in the front room were wide-plank knotty pine stained a medium brown and finished with a semi-gloss coating that reflected light without being shiny or gaudy. They were covered by thick, brightly colored area rugs with patterns that struck me as perhaps inspired or created by Native Americans.

The glass in the windows looked thick and was opaque, allowing me to see light filtered through them, but not a clear view of the outdoors. Considering there wasn't anything to see outside except snow, that made sense.

Santa pointed to a steaming mug on the

table next to the chair I chose. "I know you're on your cleanse, so this is hot chocolate made with nonfat milk and the protein powder you use after you exercise. It's actually pretty good. I may opt for it myself going forward." Santa patted his belly. "I could stand to lose a few pounds too."

I instinctively reached for the mug and smelled the "cocoa" before testing it carefully to make sure it wasn't too hot. A loud pop from the fireplace startled me, causing me to flinch and spill some of my drink down my shirt and onto my lap. Santa jumped up, grabbed a cloth napkin covered with a picture of a Christmas tree and presents, and handed it to me.

"I'm so sorry. I was sort of lost in my thoughts and the sound of the fire caused me to spill my drink." I dabbed my shirt and pants and stood to check the chair. "I don't think I got anything on your chair."

Santa replied, "Don't worry about it. I'm

sure it's fine. Sit down and let's talk. Let me know what you think of the hot chocolate."

I stuffed the napkin into the pocket of the exercise coverups I was wearing over my gym shorts, sat down, and again reached for the drink Santa had made for me. It was unbelieveably good.

"This is amazing! You *really* made it from the same protein powder I drink after I finish exercising?"

"I did, but I have to admit with all due modesty that hot chocolate made by Santa is probably different from any other because of 'Santa magic.' Still, try it yourself when you get home."

Home. His comment snapped me back to my senses. None of this was plausible.

"Okay, who the he—I mean, who are you and where am I? How is any of this really happening? *Is* it happening? Yes, you look like Santa, and this place looks like how I might imagine Santa's workshop. And you look conspicuously like Dickens's Spirit of Christmas Present. Maybe you are simply 'a fragment of underdone potato.'

"By the way, where are the elves and the reindeer? I haven't actually seen anything but this room, so I can't honestly say this place looks like Santa's workshop, can I? And, where in the world would you get the stone and wood to build this place, or applewood for the fire? We seem to be in a vast wasteland of snow and ice that is way above the tree line.

"So where am I really? I must be having a dream or a hallucination or something. What's actually being pumped into the air in the spa? Is Barry atomizing acid or something? I've never taken drugs, but this sure seems like what I would imagine a trip would be like."

Santa laughed. "Which question would you like me to answer first?"

"Your call. I'm all ears." I took another swig from the mug in my hand.

Santa said, "Fair enough. Don't get me started on Dickens. I *love* Dickens. He may be my favorite author. And Clement Moore was amazing, too, wasn't he?"

"The magic in *The Night Before Christmas* has inspired children and adults for almost two hundred years. Children listen for Santa's sleigh every Christmas Eve because of Moore's simple poem. And, reindeer are revered. Before he wrote it, most people other than Laplanders were ignorant of, or disinterested in, reindeer. Now, eating reindeer meat or drinking their blood (Did you know there was a time when some Lapps actually drank the blood of reindeer?) is frowned upon. How could anyone possibly eat one of Santa's reindeer?

"But, you and I both know Santa doesn't actually travel the globe in a sleigh pulled by eight tiny reindeer, don't we?"

I smiled and thought, *Finally, a dose of reality!*

"No, there are no elves who make toys for me. I don't fly in a sleigh. And, there actually is no Naughty List. Not even one where you are marked as an 'ass,' although maybe we should consider it in your case. Don't worry. Just kidding . . . aren't I?"

Santa laughed and his round belly actually jiggled. "That last point is important. You were worried yesterday after you remembered the message in church for maybe a nanosecond and started fuming about the guy in the truck. You think that message was simply coincidence? Well, thank God for Carol and her influence."

I almost spilled my hot chocolate again. How would he know about that? Unless he had bugged me somehow or I was dreaming, he couldn't.

"You were spot on when you talked about

the spirit of Santa. It is absolutely real. *I* am real. But, even though Santa's magic is powerful, there's no way elves could produce gifts for all the children in the world, and no way Santa could deliver all of them in one night. Santa's magic helps children dream and helps them to love and be loved. Children do that much better than most grown-ups, who too often get so caught up in what they think is important that they forget how to dream. Anyway, moms and dads help Santa do most of the rest.

"As for me, I told you I am someone who loves you. I get the dead relative thing. We can go that way if you would rather. But, I thought your choice of Santa was wonderful. It made me feel all Christmassy."

"So, you're not really Santa and I'm not at the North Pole, am I?"

"Sorry you're having trouble with this. Take another sip of your cocoa before it gets cold. Ask yourself, what is Santa?"

I took another drink and replied, "You said 'what' rather than 'who.' Why?"

"Please answer the question."

"Okay. I guess we agreed that Santa is a spirit. I suppose he is a spirit of love."

"Spot on. I couldn't have said it any better myself." He went on. "Santa isn't represented in the Bible, so some people are offended by what they consider a secular encroachment on the religious meanings of Christmas. But, maybe we can reconcile the story of Santa and the birth of Jesus as both being stories of love."

"That's nice, but none of that helps me understand why I think I'm sitting at the North Pole talking with Santa."

Santa said, "You've forgotten what we said on that first time we spoke. Lately, you've been asking for answers to a lot of questions you have. That's why we're talking. And, you asked me if we could meet, so we're meeting.

If me coming to you as Santa is bothering you, I can come as a little green man, or maybe someone in a long flowing robe with a halo, or whatever you prefer. We can even go back to a disembodied voice or a flashing light, but I don't think that is what you want, is it?"

I asked quietly, "So, you're God?"

"That question is a bridge too far for us today. I told you. I'm someone who loves you. Let's talk about where we are and how we got here. Okay?"

"I guess."

"Do you remember hearing about the astral plane when you were younger?"

"Yeah, sort of. When I was a teenager, I remember someone telling me I could have an out-of-body experience and gain access to something called the astral plane by concentrating my thoughts on moving my consciousness out of my body.

"I tried it, but the only thing I remember is having a sudden start when I was clearly aware of my surroundings after I assumed I had fallen asleep or effectively hypnotized myself. I ended up thinking it was bogus.

"Wait . . . are you suggesting the idea of astral projection is *real* and that's what is happening here? Now I understand why you thought calling Barry *Oh wow* was wrong. You're one of them."

Santa laughed at me. "You do understand you think you have every single answer to the universe, don't you? Wow, it must be amazing to be as smart as you. Finish your cocoa. I think we're done for now. See you tomorrow."

"Wait—"

In a flash, I was back in the Sea Breeze and Barry was telling me my time was up.

The whole thing was idiotic. I was positive I was simply falling asleep. I thought about asking Barry to let me review the video of my session again, but decided it wasn't worth it. No question that if I hadn't been asleep, I was out of my flippin' mind.

The gym was at the other end of the strip mall from the spa, so I drove there. I couldn't help but think that driving a few hundred feet when I was going to exercise was dumb, but rationalized it was because the wind was kind of cold and biting.

I said hi to the woman who managed the gym and she checked me in by scanning my app. Then, I found an empty locker to stash my jacket, keys, and other paraphernalia while I was exercising. I shook my head at my stupidity as I did, not able to believe how I had become wrapped up in this dream or delusion or whatever it was.

As always, I patted down my pockets to make sure I had taken out everything I didn't need while I worked out. From my left pants pocket, out came a cloth napkin with a Christmas tree and presents on it.

Seeing it in my hand, I bent over gasping for air and the manager rushed over to me to ask me if I was having a health emergency. I couldn't talk, but I tried to shake my head and wave her off.

"I'm okay. I just got dizzy. I gave blood this morning," I lied.

She said, "You shouldn't be here."

"You're right." I smiled weakly. "I think I'll go home."

She offered me some juice and asked if she could call someone for me. I told her I would be fine and merely needed to sit down for a few minutes before I drove home.

She helped me to a chair.

As I sat there, my head was exploding with questions, none of which I could answer. I knew I needed to go home and rest, and I knew I couldn't wait until tomorrow.

I was freezing the rest of the night. Carol was worried and wondered if I was getting sick. We turned up the heat in the house, but I just couldn't get warm.

TUESDAY, JANUARY 14

I decided to wear long underwear that I had bought to go skiing right after Christmas. In my case, skiing was a misnomer. I wore it to fall down in the snow before going to the bar. But, it was the latest tech and was both warm and thin. Since I wear my long exercise pants over my gym shorts until it gets too warm in the late spring, no one would notice I had them on. I also stuffed the cloth napkin back in my pocket. I'm not sure exactly why. I guess I wanted to show it to Santa when I told him what had happened to me.

Barry settled me into my chair. He was obviously pleased at this point. Not only was I a regular, I'm guessing I was quickly becoming his best customer. He even asked me if I would post something on social media. I didn't bother to tell him I think most social media is crap. Why burst his bubble?

Again, shortly after the door closed behind Barry, the bright light blinded me.

When my eyes adjusted, I saw sand instead of snow and heard the surf crashing on the shore. The sun overhead was blazing.

I *love* the ocean. The way it smells and sounds instantly lowers my blood pressure. But, why wasn't I in the cold, surrounded by snow?

The breeze was blowing the fronds on nearby palms. That is such a wonderful sound.

Then, I noticed Santa sitting in a beach chair with his bare feet in the water. It wasn't just warm; the weather was as hot as it had been cold the day before. Santa had taken off his fur-trimmed coat and his pants were rolled up almost to his knees. He had on a long-sleeved, ribbed undershirt over which were the suspenders that held up his pants. Instead of his wire-rimmed glasses, he was wearing black, horn-rimmed shades. His ensemble was topped off with a decidedly shabby straw plantation hat. In short, he looked a bit silly and out of place.

Santa was drinking something iced in a tall glass with an umbrella. He raised his glass to me in a toast and waved me over to a beach chair on his left.

I was sweating and started peeling off my long-sleeved exercise shirt. The workout pants and shorts were next, leaving me in only the long underwear I had worn in anticipation of the cold of the far north.

"What's with the beach and the heat?"

"You were cold last night, weren't you? I

know how much you like the Caribbean, so I thought we could talk here today."

"Thanks? If I had known, I would have dressed differently."

"I'll write off your prickly reaction to the fact you're hot. Have a lemonade. If you weren't on your cleanse, I'd offer you an aged amber rum, but I don't want to tempt you." Santa grinned a goofy smile.

There was something different about the way Santa looked this morning, but I couldn't put my finger on it. Maybe it was that the background had changed and he had his feet in the warm ocean, but there was something oddly familiar about him. Of course, Santa is familiar, but I didn't mean that. Still, I couldn't figure it out.

"So, the napkin helped you figure out this is actually happening and you're absolutely not dreaming or imagining everything. Right?"

I grabbed my pants and pulled out the

napkin. Staring at it, I said, "I guess so, unless I'm simply imagining I'm holding this thing."

"Tell you what, I'll sign it and date it for you. When you leave here, you can take a photo of it with your phone too. So you'll have proof it is real and you can post it on the social media you think is 'a lot of crap,' or you can frame it or do whatever you want with it. Of course, it's unlikely that anyone is going to believe how you got it, but we can talk about that later. At least *you'll* know this is real."

Santa took the napkin from me and, with sleight of hand, produced a fountain pen from somewhere. He signed it with élan and handed it back to me.

"Great. I have a napkin signed by Santa. What could be more convincing of my sanity than that?" I looked down. Just above the signature, it said, "I love you." The signature itself didn't look like it said Santa; it looked like something I hadn't seen in several years. I was confused. Being confused was starting to feel like a new normal, but without a doubt, I *knew* this signature.

Santa was again grinning at me with the goofy smile, the one that showed his teeth and gums. As he turned his head to look squarely at me, I could see the scar on the right side of his neck. I *knew* that scar. My dad was wounded very badly during World War II. The fact that he survived was a miracle. The scar on Santa's neck was exactly like Dad's, but Santa didn't have it yesterday!

"Dad?"

His goofy smile got wider.

"Dad?"

Removing his sunglasses, my dad said, "You said Santa or a dead relative. How about both?"

My dad died five years ago. Carol and I were there with him until two days before he passed. He lived close to my brother, but a seven-hour car ride away from where we lived. It was clear he was nearing the end of his life, but no one could give us any sense of when. We had spent a week with him and tried to read the tea leaves about whether he would pass shortly or linger for weeks. We talked with my brother and we talked with Dad. Both told us to go home because Carol and I had several things that needed to be done, including the fact I had work I needed to do. We told Dad we would be back in a week, but we said goodbye, just in case. 'Just in case' happened quickly.

Dad, who had been abandoned as a child and survived. Dad, who had been badly wounded during World War II and survived. Dad, who smoked and drank too much and survived . . . simply stopped breathing.

Dad, who was dead, was sitting in front of me in a Santa outfit on a beach grinning his goofy smile.

"Dad? How is this possible?"

"Still think you know all the mysteries of the universe?" Dad laughed with the wheeze I've remembered since I was a kid.

"No. I never said that."

"You didn't have to say it. You act like you have all the answers. You don't have them. You don't even know what questions to ask. But, don't let that bother you; no one else does, either. Well, that's not entirely true, is it? God does. Actually knows the answers too."

I came back with, "You weren't a big believer in God, as I recall."

"Didn't have to be. He believed in me. Or, if you prefer, She believed in me. But, I'm kind of a traditionalist. Let's go with He. Say, you want me to switch that lemonade for a twenty-year-old rum?"

Smiling, I said, "Tempting me, huh? Are you sure you're not Satan?"

Dad wheeze-laughed again. "Naw. No

such thing. But, let's wrap up some of our old business before moving to new. Remember that Santa told you there's no Naughty List?"

I nodded. "You mean, you told me as Santa, right?"

"Nope. Santa. I borrowed his outfit for today."

"Santa . . ."

"Yup. Santa. Thought you said you believed. The two of you agreed that Santa is a spirit of love. So is God. There is no Naughty List because everyone deserves to be loved. There is no Hell because no one can earn entry into Heaven. Period. Everyone is welcomed.

"There also is no Satan. The Devil was a creation of humans to explain evil and wrong. At some level, we all truly do understand the difference between right and wrong. You admitted that yourself after reading Lewis. Remember that discussion the other day? Well, people sometimes—okay, often—ignore their inner voices and commit wrongs. If you will, they sin. But, the existence of sin doesn't necessitate a devil. It only takes human frailty."

"Wow. I don't remember you ever being this deep."

"No, you thought I was foolish and you were embarrassed by me."

My face reddened and I stammered, "Yes, I was bothered by some of the things you did. We don't have to rehash them now, but you know you did things at times that were . . . odd. But, I always bragged to others that you showed me how to treat people with respect, regardless of their station in life."

"Yes, you do tell people that. But, I never saw anyone's 'station in life.' That would suggest there is some kind of hierarchy. I don't mean one based upon income or wealth or intellect. I mean one that ranks each of us based upon our value as humans.

"That's wrong. There is no ranking, because each of us is as valuable as everyone else. I failed to teach you that, so I didn't do a very good job of helping you understand the real reason for treating everyone with respect. We should do so because we are all related. We were all created in God's image—literally. We are all part of a single being that is pure love."

I shook my head. "It's great to be sitting here seeing you and talking with you, *if* I truly am, and this philosophical discussion is interesting, but you or Santa or the 'Great Oz' told me the reason for these conversations was about my questions about Reagan getting cancer. What does all of this have to do with that?

"And, Santa promised to tell me more about astral projection. I'm supposed to believe astral projection is a gateway to another dimension? Heaven? As fantastic as that would be, I'm not swallowing it. I need more to convince me before I'm ready to sign off on something as incredible as that."

"You've always been a tough sell, haven't you? Your questions about Reagan are exactly why we're talking. You simply have yet to connect the dots. You will."

Dad went on. "But, you were right to be embarrassed when I tried to date a nineteen-year-old after your mother died, or when I wasted a lot of money gambling and taking outrageously extravagant trips I couldn't pay for, or when I got stinking drunk or did any of the other things I did that were wrong. I didn't listen to my inner voice because it stopped talking to me years earlier. I also wouldn't listen to you or your brother. I'm sorry.

"I sure wish I could have gone on that boat of yours." Carol and I had bought a nice deck boat when we moved to our home in Georgia. "But when I came to see you, I embarrassed you because I didn't pack clothes or the adult diapers I needed and I soiled myself on the plane. I'm sorry."

"That isn't why, Dad! You couldn't walk well enough to get down the steps to the boat, or into and out of it. And there's no way we could have gotten you back up to the house from the boat."

What I had said was honest and true, but so was Dad's comment about how I had felt about him. I had been disgusted by what I saw as his total lack of self-respect. Looking at Dad now, I was more embarrassed, but of myself, not by him. I saw myself as shallow and self-absorbed—a legend in my own mind. By seeing Dad as I did on that beach, I recognized how small and weak and flawed I am.

Dad smiled at me, but this time it wasn't goofy. "We all do things that embarrass us. They bother us because we *do* know right from wrong. Sometimes we don't see the problem at first, but we eventually do. The good news is we can forgive ourselves and each other because God forgives us.

"That's pretty much what I came here to say today. The sun is going to set in another fifteen minutes or so. How about we just sit here and enjoy it? Don't worry about the spa. Time here passes differently than it does in that dimension."

We sat in silence and watched the sun approach the horizon.

"Dad . . . what's it like? Being dead. Heaven, I guess."

"I'm not sure I can answer that in a way you will understand. I'm not trying to insult you. It's simply difficult for people to understand it while they're alive." He paused for a minute, looking hard into the distance, then turned back to me. "You know what it's like on a really foggy morning when you can't see your hand in front of your face?"

I nodded, thinking he was telling me that everything in Heaven is hazy and confusing.

He finished his illustration. "It's like the moment when that fog suddenly lifts and everything is clear and bright and sparkling in front of you. It's amazing. But, you need to wait for it. Don't rush your life, or you won't fully appreciate it when the fog clears."

I had never been so impressed with him, and I realized the fault had been mine, not his.

The sun sank into the ocean, with only the red-orange aura remaining slightly above the horizon. Suddenly, there was a jade-green flash and I was back in the Sea Breeze.

I wished I had told my dad I was wrong. Yes, some of the things he did . . . well, a lot of the things he did bothered me. But, he was a good soul and I didn't treat him with the love and respect I should have.

Rummaging in my pocket, I found the napkin with his message of love. I should have told him I loved him. I'll tell him when I see him tomorrow, and I'll ask him about Mom.

What if this astral plane thing isn't a fantasy, but in fact a gateway of some kind connecting this world with another? It would be incredible! If it is, I wonder if Dad knows any of the people in history who fascinate me? Maybe he could arrange to introduce me to Teddy Roosevelt or Lincoln! I can't wait to see him and talk with him some more so I can try to better understand how all of this works.

This whole thing is far more than strange, but the potential is staggeringly interesting at the same time. The possibilities for discovery are amazing . . . unless I'm really just nuts.

WEDNESDAY, JANUARY 15

I went to the spa at the usual time today and waited. Nothing happened. I don't know why. No Dad. No Santa. No nothing. Is that it? Is it over? Why?

There were so many questions I should have asked, but didn't. I'm not sure why I hadn't. Maybe it was that I had spent too much time worrying about whether what was happening was real that I had simply blown a great opportunity.

If that's it and there aren't going to be any other conversations, what did I learn?

I can be a jerk.

That's not a revelation to me. I know it and I keep working on me ... with little success, but I do try. Scarlett O'Hara was right. "Tomorrow is another day." I get another chance to be better tomorrow and every tomorrow after that. I'll screw up. That's not an excuse, just a fact. Still, I'll keep trying to learn from my mistakes and get better.

No Naughty List.

Well, I guess that makes sense, especially if Santa is a representation of love. Kids ... adults, too, do things that are wrong, but that doesn't mean they should be unloved. I have to admit, this one is hard for me. This is one I wish I had asked more about. I'm not talking about someone screwing up something by accident or maybe even on purpose. I mean someone who is truly evil. Is it wrong to punish someone for doing evil things?

I want to understand why Reagan got cancer.

To say, "That sucks," doesn't begin to capture what I feel. Yet, my questioning is apparently what started all these crazy events over the last several days. I want an answer that is more than "because."

My dad sorta looks like Santa.

Never noticed it before.

I like the sun and the beach a lot more than the cold and the snow.

Wait . . . I already knew that.

This astral plane thing may really exist, or I may be crazy.

Let's go with the astral plane.

I wish I had asked more questions about what happens after we die. Dad described it like coming out of a deep fog.

I should have listened to my dad more when I had the chance.

Salt spas aren't bad. I shouldn't call people names. Barry's okay.

I don't dislike salt, but I don't use too much of it. I like pepper. Why couldn't Sea Breeze be a pepper spa?

I'm not talking about any of this to anyone.

I was surprised by how sad I am nothing happened. A few days ago, the idea of nothing happening seemed pretty good. But now?

Barry asked me if I wanted the same time as usual for tomorrow. He was disappointed when I told him I was feeling better and didn't want to book anything right then. So much for being a regular. But, I gave him a bright smile and waved as I said, "See you soon." I didn't mean it.

When I got home, Carol had done laundry, folded it, and left my things on our bed for me to put away. It was at that moment I remembered I had thrown my exercise coverups into the dirty clothes yesterday. I had sat in something. Didn't matter; I had three pairs, even if these were my favorites.

But the napkin with the message from Dad had been in the pocket! I grabbed the pants and struggled to unzip the pocket, which for some reason was stuck. As I pulled out the napkin, I saw the reds and greens from the tree and presents had bled. Worse, the ink had smeared into an illegible mess.

I stared at it and started to get mad at Carol. She should have checked my pockets!

I stopped. No, she shouldn't have. It wasn't her fault. It was mine. I should have taken the napkin out of my pocket before throwing my pants into the dirty laundry.

I sat down and held the napkin close, and silently cried.

I'm not sure how much time passed before I knew what I needed to do.

Barry was happy to hear my voice and was glad to confirm my session for tomorrow morning, but he was sorry I had a sinus headache again so soon.

There are no coincidences. What will tomorrow bring?

THURSDAY, JANUARY 16

Shortly after Barry left me in the salt cave, I felt myself transported to a strange place—as if anything could be strange after what I had been experiencing for the last week. But, it wasn't strange in the sense of being odd, just unfamiliar.

I was on a narrow, uneven, cobblestoned street bordered by row houses of three or four stories. It was night and the chilled air was thick with fog. Gas lamps dimly shone through the mist. From what I could make out, the homes were brick and stone. Their darkened windows were largely shuttered. In the distance, I could hear what sounded like a horse clip-clopping on the pavement. Otherwise, there was a total absence of sound. I had absolutely no idea where I was.

As I peered into the haze, I saw movement in the distance. A figure, silhouetted by one of the streetlights, was walking toward me. I tensed.

Coming closer, I saw the stranger was a man who appeared to be perhaps fifty. His greying, curly hair was thinning on the top and he sported an unruly mustache and long chin whiskers. He had a walking stick in hand and his clothes were like something out of a public television film set in London in the mid-nineteenth century.

The approaching man extended a hand as he neared me. "Tom—may I call you Tom? It is so very good to meet you." His accent was decidedly British. I was more confused than I had been in any of my earlier encounters. At least when I met Santa (wow, I was actually thinking of him as Santa) and my dad, they had been familiar to me. This person seemed to know me, but I had no clue who he was.

I tentatively took his hand. "I'm sorry. You clearly were expecting me, but I'm afraid I don't know who you are. I thought I was going to meet my dad."

"Of course. Forgive me. I'm sorry your father isn't here. My name is Charles Dickens. I understand you have read several of my works. I'm flattered."

I don't know why meeting someone who claimed to be Charles Dickens would shock me more than Santa or my dead father, but for some reason, it did.

"Charles Dickens? As in *the* Charles Dickens? How in the . . . Why in the . . . It's nice to meet you. I'm a huge fan."

"I am honored."

"I'm sorry. Where are we?"

"Why, London, of course."

"London. What year is it?"

"I believe it is 1859, but that isn't important. Time for us is merely a convenience. It helps provide us with a foundation for our meeting. However, your present day is more than one hundred and fifty years distant from where we are right now. I am but a spirit in your time, yet I was very much alive in 1859. I thought meeting in my time would aid our conversation, if that is agreeable to you."

I nodded weakly, more bewildered than ever.

"May I suggest we get out of the chill of the night? My home is nearby. We will be much more comfortable there."

Without waiting for me to respond, Dickens took me by the arm and led me to an impressive townhome. We went up the front steps and entered.

He directed us to what appeared to be the

parlor, stoked the fireplace embers to provide some additional warmth, and lit a lantern on a table before settling us into comfortable wingback chairs.

Looking around, I saw oils of what I assumed to be his family hanging at a level that would be too high on the walls in the twenty-first century. A heavy brass rod held a large tapestry as well. The walls themselves were covered by paper that reminded me of the wallpaper patterns Carol had liked when we were younger.

Dickens said, "I believe you are in the middle of what you refer to as a cleanse, but are you certain you can't make an exception? I would be happy to get you a port or a glass of sherry."

"No. Thank you." This was surreal. I was sitting with Charles Dickens! He certainly wasn't Teddy or Lincoln, but he sure was an historical figure.

"I am certain you are wondering why the two of us are meeting."

"Yes. Well, I assumed it may be because of my interest in history, and I had wondered about the possibility of meeting an important historical figure. You are absolutely an important figure from the past . . . at least from the past as I know it."

"Well, thank you for the compliment, but I am not here to enlighten you on historical events—at least not those that may be somewhat familiar to you. I am here because I know some of what you have been recently experiencing, and I want to share with you how I happened to write *A Christmas Carol*."

"Really! That book is such a classic. I've read it several times, and there have been many, many films produced that tell your story, as well as numerous other writers and artists who have 'borrowed' your work as inspiration."

I leaned forward. "I remember reading that when you were young, you yourself actually experienced many of the financial challenges your characters often did."

"I did. My early years heavily influenced my writing."

"I can see that also in Bob Cratchit and his family. But, how did you come up with Scrooge and the three ghosts? It was brilliant, and your descriptions were captivating. Your writing always makes me want to strive to be a better person."

"Again, thank you. But, you grant me more credit than I am due."

"I'm sorry. I don't understand."

"You see, like you, I was searching for answers in my life. By 1843, my wife, Catherine, and I had four children. We would eventually have ten. I was already quite successful. Queen Victoria herself read my stories.

"But I was lost. I had experienced suffering as a youth and saw it all around me. And I had enjoyed success. Why? Why me when so many others were not able to rise above the fray? The answer came to me in the same way it has come to you. I wrote *A Christmas Carol* because I was quite literally visited by spirits, as you have been."

I caught my breath. "What? You're not serious! Are you suggesting the events you wrote about were inspired by something that *actually* happened to you?"

"Not inspired, sir. I am telling you I simply wrote what truly happened and merely changed the names to protect me from the criticism that would have come if I had told the world I was not writing a fiction. No, that itself is a fiction, isn't it? I wouldn't have simply been criticized. I would have been confined in Bedlam.

"My editor was amazed I had written *A*

Christmas Carol in only six weeks. I didn't. I wrote it in about ten days once I decided to tell my story. Of course, I fittingly played the part of Scrooge himself."

I jumped out of my chair. "You have gone through what I have? That's amazing!"

"Yes, it is. You and I have both been blessed. We both asked for answers to important life questions, and those answers were granted to us in a unique way. But, a word of caution—and that's why I am talking with you, why we are meeting—"

I interrupted Dickens. "I can't believe this sort of thing happened to both of us!"

"Ah, it happens more often than you think."

"I don't understand. You mean that it's common for the living world and the spirit worlds to communicate?"

"Yes, of course. The veil that separates the two is thin indeed. But, far more often than not, the living miss or simply ignore those messages.

"In fairness, the contacts are more typically subtle, much more so than what you and I have shared. It may simply be that a bit of seeming intuition that is the footprint of the communication. Or, it may be a dream. And, I'm certain you have looked at a figure in a cloud, or noticed someone staring back at you as you examine the pattern in a marble slab. That isn't your imagination. Someone is truly staring back at you—from another world.

"Yes, most of these contacts are merely dismissed. But, make no mistake, it happens all the time. What we choose to do with those messages is up to us.

"As I started to say a moment ago, Ebenezer Scrooge was changed by his experience. I am sad to say I was not. Please, don't misconstrue what I am telling you. I was changed at first. But, I quickly forgot what I had learned. What I had been shown.

"Tom, I was not a nice person. I grew tired

of my children. I treated my wife badly, having multiple lovers before I left her in 1858. I turned my back on those I should have held dear, and while many of my literary characters still displayed exemplary human qualities, far too often I did not.

"But time wounds all heals." Dickens offered a tight smile. "I was ill the last five years of my life and died at age fifty-eight. What did my fame and fortune gain me? In the end, nothing. I squandered all the many blessings I received. Jacob Marley warned Scrooge how he should live his life. I am giving you the same advice. And, that is why we are meeting."

I protested. "I'm sorry, sir. I don't quite understand. I have no intention of leaving my wife or treating her badly. Why are you telling me this?"

"Because, it is not only your wife who is important. Yes, love her and care for her. But, as Marley said, 'Mankind should have been my business.' It should be yours, as well. 'Love one another, as I have loved you.' Heed that and live by it. Everything else will, in turn, follow."

"I don't get it. I came to London in the 1850s to hear the same sermon I heard at church last week—from Charles Dickens, no less? Why?"

"Because you said you wanted to talk."

With that, I was back at the Sea Breeze. I shook my head, unable to think clearly. I just couldn't fully comprehend what was going on. Why the repeated message? Yes, I admit I had gotten pissed at God because Reagan had been diagnosed with cancer, and I wanted to try to delve more into the meaning of life—into its purpose.

I also agree my experiences so far have embarrassed me and given me a reason to reexamine my life and how I treat others. But a Dickensian intervention—one that included a supposed confession that he had actually been "visited" by spirits?

Again, maybe I'm simply crazy. Or, if I really did meet Charles Dickens, maybe he was crazy too. I have no idea what to expect next. I'm thinking this would be a good time to end my cleanse.

I didn't. If I had started drinking, there's no telling when I would have stopped.

FRIDAY, JANUARY 17

Okay, today was the weirdest of all these stupid days since things stopped being normal. It made me wish I could turn back the calendar to when my only complaints would be my dumb decisions about which stocks to buy or sell and when.

I greeted Barry with a smile. He looked a little down, so I asked him if something was bothering him. He shared with me that business was slower than he would like, but he smiled and said he hoped things would pick up in the spring as the weather started to get warm and people began to be more active.

I said I assumed the pine pollen would cause a lot of people to have allergic reactions that would end up being good for business. The thought made him beam expectantly. I've cursed that yellow coating ever since Carol and I moved to Georgia, never thinking pollen could benefit someone.

Until the pines starting dusting everything in sight, I had a feeling my visits might, unfortunately, be a significant part of Barry's bookings. Somehow that realization made me sad and concerned for him.

I settled into my usual chair in the salt cave and waited for my next adventure into *The Twilight Zone.*

True to form, I was transported, this time to what reminded me of a fun, sci-fi-themed cantina Carol and I had been to a couple of weeks before Christmas. I thought it was very cool, so maybe that's why I was now someplace that looked like I remembered it.

Strange music was playing softly in the background, but the place was empty— except for one other. Sitting at a round table away from the bar was the prototypical little green man . . . person . . . being of some kind. He/it stood and waved me over.

At full height, it appeared to be perhaps four and a half feet tall with a head that seemed to come directly out of its shoulders and long skinny arms that hung down almost to its knees.

It was dressed in a loose khaki tunic and olive cargo pants that were stuffed into black boots. It had no hair, long ears, bulging eyes, an upturned nose, and its face was a mass of wrinkles. It sort of reminded me of a hairless, green Shar-Pei. Not a pretty sight.

"Hi, Tom. Just when you thought you had seen it all, I show up." It laughed at what it apparently considered to have been a clever comment. "I'm called Pug." It laughed again. "Ironic, huh?"

"Nice to meet you, Pug. At least, I think it's nice to meet you. Is Pug a guy's name or a woman's?"

"Depends."

"Okay, depends upon what?"

"Whether it is a male or a female who has it." Once more, Pug laughed.

"Right. So, why are we meeting, and where in the world are we?"

"Well, not in the world—at least not yours. But, that isn't important." Pug continued, "You seemed open to little green men and you wanted to talk. So, let's talk."

"Since I'm now convinced that there's no question I'm going to be committed, what is it you want to share with me that will help me better understand God, the universe, and why my daughter has cancer?"

"Sorry about your daughter. By that, I mean I'm sorry her having cancer is hard for you and hard for her. I understand she's coping better than you are. But, I'm not here to talk about your daughter."

"Why the hell not? That's what made me start this whole thing . . . at least, it started me asking questions."

"It isn't that I don't care about you or your daughter. It's not my job to answer those questions for you. What I am here to do is to share with you that the universe is far more incredible than you or any of the rest of us can understand until we stand face to face with God."

"You believe in God?"

"Absolutely not."

"Then why are we here?"

"I don't believe in God. I *know* God. God isn't an imaginary being who was created by our ancestors. God is real, and He plays an important role in our lives. He created all of us and we are all part of Him."

"I'm sorry. God created you *and* me . . . in His image? I don't have a mirror, but you and I don't exactly look alike."

Pug mocked me. "What? Now you tell me. I was told you were full of yourself, but I was also told you were sort of smart. I get the first part of that, but I'm not too sure about the second. You seem to have a particularly narrow concept of God. You don't think God is really a human man, do you? Probably a white guy, huh?"

"Well, no. He could be a woman, I guess. And, I didn't say He is white. He could be any color."

"Just not someone green."

"I didn't say that! You're putting words into my mouth."

"I can't do that now. It's too full with your foot in it."

Pug was right. "Look. I'm sorry. We got off to a rocky start and it's my fault. Can we try again?"

Smiling, Pug's face wrinkled still more. "Nice pivot. Apology accepted. Maybe it makes sense to begin at the beginning.

"We are all created by God. Our superficial differences don't make us actually different. We simply all are intended to play a part in God's symphony and He is the leader of the band. So, you and I come from different parts of the universe that are separated by billions of light years, but we are one and we need each other. How we need each other isn't clear to us now, but it is to God. There's nothing wrong with asking why. The only thing that is problematic is when we act contrary to Jesus's command and fail to love one another."

"So, you know Christ too? He came to your planet—to your part of the universe?"

"Yes and no. God sent Christ to earth."

"As the son of God."

"The Bible tells us that 'God so loved the earth that he sent his only begotten son.' You are the son of God. We are all sons and daughters of God. So, absolutely, Christ came to earth as the son of God with a message: love one another." Pug continued while I tried to grasp what he had said.

"But, it is perhaps a mistake of human arrogance to assume God would only come to earth to share his message, and to only do so once. God is talking with us constantly and in many ways—ways each of us can understand if we try."

Pug pulled what looked like a dog biscuit out of a pocket in his tunic and began enthusiastically chomping on it.

"On earth, God sent you Jesus, but God is way too smart to rely solely upon one way of communicating. God didn't send a human to my neighborhood. How do you think that would have gone over? Still, that doesn't mean He didn't come to us with the same message. He just did so in a way we could understand.

"Broaden your thinking a bit. God talks to us and wants us to talk back. Say, you're probably good at the talking back part, aren't you? As with the others, I am only a messenger here to help prep you—"

I didn't let Pug finish. "Prep me for what?"

"Wow, you are a handful, aren't you? I'm here to, hopefully, open your mind so you can ask the right questions and actually listen to the answers. You sure didn't listen last week in church. That message didn't even stick with you long enough to get you out of the parking lot."

"All right, I get it! I'm an ass. I've been told that regularly over the last week. I admit it."

Pug growled, "No, you're not! You *act* like an ass sometimes—well, a lot. But, you have a tremendous spirit. Believe me, I can smell the good in you. I mean it! My nose is amazing. By the way, I think you should cut back on the garlic. I know you think it is good for your cleanse, but trust me, you don't need as much as you're taking.

"You have the ability to share your God-given goodness much more with others if you can only accept the fact that we are all one— yes, even you and I are one. If you can only stop worrying about being judged and judging others, you will find more joy in this life and the next."

"Okay, okay. Stop barking orders at me." That drew yet another laugh from Pug. "I get the message. So, how many more 'ghosts' do I have to meet? Scrooge only had three, and he got to wrap things up in one night. You're my fourth visitation, if you don't count the 'Great Oz.' This is starting to feel like *Groundhog Day*, except my day changes more."

"Good analogy. You'll keep meeting another spirit each day until you actually do get the message. You think you have it now, but you don't."

"Great. Glad to hear it," I said, "Beam me up, Scotty. I'm outta here."

I jumped as Barry gently tapped me on my shoulder. "I think you fell asleep today, Tom. You were mumbling something like you were talking with someone in another world."

My head cleared. "You have no idea. I know I haven't been planning on doing a treatment on Saturday, but do you have an opening tomorrow morning?"

Barry was only too happy to book my appointment.

SATURDAY, JANUARY 18

The door clicked behind Barry and I was immediately in Cuppa sitting across the table from Sally. A steaming cup of tea sat in front of me in a porcelain mug, exactly the way I liked it. No one else was there.

"Sally?"

"Hi, Tom. I'm so glad to see you."

"I don't get it. Cuppa? Where is everyone?"

Sally replied, "Well, we're not really in Cuppa, are we? It's just a representation of a familiar place for us. It's where we met."

I rapped my knuckles hard on the table.

"Well, this representation seems real enough to me. This table is solid, and I hurt myself when I hit it." I grabbed the tea and took a long pull. It was way too hot for me to have done that. "Ow! And, I burned my mouth on this blasted representation of a cup of tea."

"I didn't say none of this is real. I simply said we're not really in Cuppa. At least, we're not where we actually met."

Sally was smiling at me like I was a child who didn't understand adult things.

"Well, where are we? You're not a dead relative or Santa or someone who loves me, and you're certainly not green. Why are you here?"

"Green? Well, all good questions. Let's see if I can help. This representation is as real as Santa's workshop or the beach. It is real for you. The astral plane does kind of work like a gateway. (I think you were asking that, weren't you?) But let's come back to that in a minute."

"I'm here because you wanted to talk about Reagan. I have some experience with that sort of thing. So, maybe I can help. Yes, I'm Sally, but not exactly the Sally you met. It might be easier for you to think of me as her spirit. Her soul, if you will."

"What? How . . . how could you coexist?"

"Remember when you spent time asking yourself whether you were ready to commit to marriage before you proposed to Carol? You were twenty-one, weren't you? You have always laughed and told people you must have been visited by your older self. Otherwise, you said, you weren't smart enough at that time to come up with the answers that made you get down on one knee.

"You said that a couple of days before you proposed, you realized new relationships give people that warm and fuzzy feeling. As the newness wears off, people have to keep working on keeping the relationship new or the grass will always be greener. People who don't understand that will always be chasing after the giddiness of something new. You said relationships take work. You've done a good job of remembering that with Carol. It's easy to see the two of you are in love.

"You also said you didn't just want to be with the beautiful young woman she was, but with the older woman she would become, so you could share a lifetime of memories with her. Again, the two of you are a match made in heaven. Promise!

"And you were right, you weren't that wise. Yet. You *were* visited by your older self. Well, you were visited by your spirit that is as real as you are."

I shook my head. "So, you're telling me I exist—we all exist—on more than one plane at the same time? What happens when we die and the two come together? Do we vaporize like matter and anti-matter colliding? This sounds like a load of crap."

Sally laughed. "No, silly. Your spirit is always with you. It is that voice you sometimes ignore. You aren't two different entities. You're simply much more special than you think. You were made that way. We all are.

"We try to understand these things while we're living, but we do so with varying degrees of success. Heaven gives us the opportunity to see things much more clearly. Your dad's description of a fog lifting was a brilliant way to try to help you understand that.

"The astral plane is really a reference to a merging of your conscious thoughts with your spirit. And, as you achieve that (to the extent you can), it is possible to connect with the spirits of others because we are all truly interrelated. Your dad suggested that when he talked about us all being part of a single being that is pure love.

"Think of being connected as being a part of a team. I know that's simplistic, but it works if you'll bear with me for a minute. What happens to a quarterback in football if the line doesn't block for him?"

"He gets creamed."

"Right. I can give you any number of different analogies, but they all have the same outcome. We weren't created as separate, independent entities. We are all very much dependent upon each other. It just isn't always easy to understand that."

Sally paused, looked deeply into my eyes, and asked, "What did your pastor say Jesus asked his followers to do?"

"Love each other as I have loved you?"

Clapping, she said, "Exactly! Love each other because we all are one."

I pushed back. "BS. I mean, I heard what he said, but there have to be limits. Plenty of people are *really bad* people. I'm not buying the idea that God created bad people as part of this one entity, and I'm not buying that a loving God would give my little girl cancer."

Sally smiled wider. "God didn't create any bad people. People sometimes do bad things. Eventually, they will understand that, but it may be in their next life."

I slammed my fist down on the table. "So, that's it. Do whatever you want and don't worry about it. You're forgiven. Bull!"

"Can you imagine the fog lifting and truly understanding the harm you did to others during your life? There is no Hell, per se. God forgives everything and everyone, but all of our harsh words and deeds are before us in the next world. That's what Dickens was really trying to tell us when Jacob Marley came to visit Scrooge, trailing a chain that represented the wrongs he had committed—his sins, if you will, while he was alive.

"As for Reagan, even at forty, she's your

little girl, isn't she? God did *not* give your daughter cancer. Full stop. It doesn't work like that. God doesn't look to reward some people and punish others. We are all loved the same.

"But, God does work in mysterious ways. Reagan has cancer. You reached out to talk. At the same time, Reagan, who had lost her faith, has begun looking for answers as well. Again, God, who sees the past, present, and future at the same time, didn't give Reagan cancer, but he knew she would have it. He also knew the two of you would reach out to talk.

"And I am here because I am blessed to know so many children who are very ill, most of whom won't get better. I'm not telling you Reagan won't recover. Don't read anything into me being here other than the fact that I care."

I said, "When I originally asked who the voice was at the salt spa, the answer was 'someone who loves you.' I'll accept that you're a very nice person, but someone who loves me?"

"Again, we're all in this together. We are all one. Each of us who is connecting with you loves you. Remember, 'love one another as I have loved you.'"

I looked at Sally. "Wow. This is pretty heavy—especially for Cuppa."

Sally laughed. "Not really. I know this all sounds 'out there' to you, but we're talking about life. Most of us know at a deep level that we all need each other and that we should treat each other with kindness. We sometimes get too distracted by what's going on in our daily lives and we forget. All of us need to do better."

I hung my head briefly, then looked up. "I'm sorry about how I treated you the last time we met."

She grinned. "Thank you! See, you're

actually good at this 'one for all and all for one' thing when you're focused on it."

I gave her a crooked smile. "Not really. Carol is good at it. I have a long way to go."

"We all do." Sally added, "Your cup's empty. Let's call it a day."

"Sally, I'm so glad you were the one to come to me today. I mean that. I heard what you said about God not rewarding and not punishing people, but I still struggle with a God who loves us yet lets bad things happen to good people. Well, people, I guess, if I accept your comment that there are no 'bad' people—even though I am not sure I can fully buy that. So, I guess I'll have to keep working at it and wait for what tomorrow brings. Am I going to meet God?"

"I didn't say that. You said you wanted to talk with God. Since we're all created in God's image, in a way, every one of us, the spirits you meet, is a little like talking with

God. Of course, the same is true in life, isn't it?"

The power of Sally's last comment hung in the air as I let it soak in.

"But, I'm sorry to tell you I don't know for sure who's next on your dance card. I guess you'll have to wait to find out."

I went straight to the "real" Cuppa from the Sea Breeze hoping Sally would be there. She wasn't. I was disappointed. Before heading home, I ordered a tea and went to the toilet. When I came out of the john, Sally was just coming into the restaurant! I went up to her and apologized for being an ass last week. Sally blushed and told me she hadn't noticed anything. Instead, she again said she was sorry for being slow to order. Amazing. When I asked, Sally was kind enough to let me buy her a coffee. We sat and talked. She's a wonderfully interesting person.

Taking the time to meet Sally and to get to know her a little more was something new for me. It wasn't much of a start on my road to a better me, but, "The longest journey . . ."

I stayed at Cuppa to record my notes for the day and grabbed a latte to take home to Carol. At some point, I'm going to have to tell her what's been happening. I'm just not sure how she's going to react.

WEDNESDAY, JANUARY 22

I've been kissed before, but she was kissing me all over my face, so much that I reached up a hand to wipe off the saliva.

Opening my eyes slowly, I saw two big brown eyes staring back at me. She wiggled on my chest and let out a yip before going back to kissing me.

I felt a little like I was swimming in mud. My tongue was thick and dry and my ears were ringing. But I managed to croak out, "Trudy?"

Trudy stopped for a second to look at me

before lunging back at my face to cover me with wet kisses.

"What are you doing here? You've been gone for what—seven years?"

Carol had found Trudy almost eighteen years ago. She was shy and a momma's girl. The other pups in her litter were wild and very energetic. Carol liked the way Trudy hung back from the others. She said she would be less independent and bond with us more quickly.

Carol was spot on. From the first day we brought her home, Trudy had slept in our bed and wanted to be near us.

I wasn't keen on having her in our bed, at first. I was sure she would pee in it. Carol told me there was nothing to worry about because she wouldn't pee where she was sleeping. Once again, she was right.

Trudy's formal name was Gertrude, fitting for her German heritage, but she was always just Trudy to us.

Carol has a passion for dachshunds, but she is very specific on what she likes. When she decided to look for a dog, she wanted a miniature, not a toy (too small) or a standard (too big). It was a Goldilocks thing, I guess. It had to be a reddish-brown. Black markings were a plus, as long as it was red-brown with black and not black with red-brown. The snout had to be on the short side. Long, pointy noses were definitely out. And, it had to be a female. No little male dogs for my Carol.

Turdy certainly fit the bill to a tee. The black markings on her ears and back faded as she matured, but she sure had them when she was a puppy.

The Trudy that was loving on me again had her black markings. But, that wasn't as strange as the fact she had died before we moved to Georgia. That was six years ago, so I figured she had been gone almost seven.

When I reached out to hug her, I saw there were tubes attached to my right hand. My eyes followed the tubes to the IV drip slowly giving me fluids. A blood pressure cuff was wrapped around my other arm and a machine was beeping rhythmically from somewhere behind me. That's when I also became acutely aware of the fact my head hurt. I mean *hurt*, like an eleven on a ten-point scale. The only thing curious about that was I hadn't noticed it when I first awoke. I guess seeing Trudy had distracted me. But, it sure hurt now.

I was obviously in a hospital, but I had no idea how I had gotten there or why.

I looked for a call button for the nurse. Maybe some pain meds would help. Before I could ring for assistance, someone from around the foot of my bed spoke to me.

"Man, you are sure gettin' some lovin'."

Peering around Trudy, who was blocking

my view of the person talking with me, I saw a round black woman with a gap-toothed grin and graying hair that was cropped short. She was wearing blue hospital scrubs, so I assumed she might be my nurse.

Hearing the nurse, Trudy paused her kisses and bounded toward her, yipping and whining like the nurse was an old friend. My nurse bent over, put her hand under Trudy's snout, tilted her head upward, and nuzzled Trudy. "How are ya, sweetheart?"

Trudy welcomed the affection, then dashed back to me. I had to hold her at bay so I could speak with the nurse.

"I didn't think dogs were allowed to be in hospitals."

"They usually aren't, darlin', but we'll make an exception this time. How ya feelin'?"

"My head hurts. Can I get something for it?"

"Of course, sugar."

My nurse came up to me, glanced at the monitor above me, looked at my eyes, and put her hand on my forehead. The pain was immediately gone.

"How did you do that? What did you do? You didn't give me anything in my IV. You touched my forehead and it stopped hurting!

"I'm so glad."

I looked for my nurse's nametag, but didn't see one. "I'm sorry, what is your name?"

"Whatever you would like it to be, honey."

"What?"

"Why don't you call me Rose?"

"Your name is Rose, then."

"Uh-huh. It is now."

"What does that mean?"

"It means you can call me Rose."

"Okay, Rose. Where am I? I mean, I can see I'm in the hospital, but why? What in the world happened?"

"What's the last thing you remember?"

I squinted my eyes, trying to remember anything. "Not much. I met someone at Cuppa. Then, I bought a latte for my wife, Carol, and took it home. That's it."

"Well, darlin', you didn't get home. There was an accident. You were stopped at a light when a man in an SUV went into insulin shock. He hit you from behind at almost sixty without touching the brakes. The impact drove you into the car in front of you and that car was pushed into the intersection, where it was hit by a semi that was on the cross-street.

"You hit your head pretty good and were rushed here to the hospital. The CT showed you had a concussion, and it also showed something else. You had a tumor on your brain." My pulse quickened. "Now, don't you worry about that, because it turned out to be benign. The doctors removed it successfully. But, because of swelling on your brain as a result of the accident and the compounding stress related to the surgery, the docs decided to induce a coma to limit the swelling."

"A *tumor*? You're not kidding me, are you? I actually wondered whether I had something like that. I don't believe it!"

"Do I look like I'm kidding, honey?"

"No, I suppose you don't." I thought about my car. "My car! I babied it. Must have been totaled. Ugh."

"Sure was."

"What happened to the others who were in the accident?"

"Wasn't your first thought, was it? The man with diabetes was treated and released. The other person wasn't so lucky. He died at the scene."

"I'm sorry."

"You may remember him. The boy who got the speeding ticket a few days ago, Andy. He passed your car and slipped in front of you before the light changed. Otherwise, you would have been the one pushed into the intersection."

"Oh, no. That's so sad. I didn't know him, but I did hear a bit of his story." I realized something was out of place. "Wait a minute. How did you know I knew about Andy? What's going on here?"

Rose laughed at me. "Don't get yourself all worked up, sweetheart. We don't need your BP to spike like it is."

A man's voice interrupted. "Have I come at a bad time?"

I turned my focus toward the voice, and seeing Andy, I started to make a muffled scream like someone having a bad dream.

Rose put her hand on my arm. It was an instant sedative. "You're all right, sugar. I'm with you."

I looked at Rose, then Andy, then back at Rose. "You said Andy died, but he's standing here."

"Yes, he did, and yes, he is."

"Then I'm dead too?"

"No, of course not, honey. Didn't you hear me tell you that you survived? In fact, that accident actually *saved* your life because it let the doctors find the tumor in your brain. You're just fine."

"I don't understand."

Rose laughed. "I would have thought you would be used to being visited by spirits by now. Remember that Andy here wanted to study to be a vet? Well, he didn't get to do that, but he's going to help me take care of the animals here. We have a lot of them."

"You have a lot of them where?"

"Why, in Heaven, darlin'. Where do you think?"

"Dogs . . . in Heaven . . ."

"Now, I know you saw the movie. *All* dogs go to Heaven. Who do you think helped them with the script?"

"That accident and/or the tumor must have done more damage than the doctors think. I'm hallucinating. I dreamed up this whole thing for what seemed like days and I'm still in it."

"Why do you think that?"

"Because I can't be in Heaven if I'm not dead, and I can't have been talking with Santa or my father or any of the rest of the people I thought I met." Trudy found her way to Andy and he was now holding her. "And my dead dog isn't here, either. This is nuts. No, it is merely an illusion caused by whatever drugs I'm being given."

"I know you are still having trouble with all of this, but I promise you, sugar, this is as real as it gets."

I looked at Rose. "So, you're Rose, or are you God?"

Rose smiled. "I can be whoever you want me to be." With that, her appearance changed into Santa, my dad, Dickens, Pug, and Sally in rapid succession before returning to Rose. She pulled a chair up to my bed and took my hand. "Let's have that talk."

"This can't be happening."

"Why not, honey?"

"Because, people don't just have a talk with God!"

"Well, that's not really right, is it? What do you think prayer is?

"Okay, but that's not the same as holding God's hand and staring into Her face!"

Rose laughed. "Not exactly. I'll give you that, but I'm happy to talk with everyone at any time. Most don't ask like you did.

"Now, you're thinking that talking with God is crazy. Why? I know you have noticed some of the miracles of the universe. You have told Carol how awed you are by things around you. Love may be my best miracle. I love you. You wanted to talk, so let's talk."

Questions started flying through my head. "So, let's start with Reagan. Why did she get cancer?"

"Sally did a good job of answering that one for you, but we can talk about it again. God doesn't let things happen or keep them from happening. You were given free will. Life isn't predetermined. What is important is what people do when something happens that they are either happy or unhappy about.

"Reagan being diagnosed with cancer is why she has started talking with me and why you have as well. Remember that there are no coincidences. If you hadn't reached out, you wouldn't have met Sally at Cuppa last week, wouldn't have been in the accident, and the doctors wouldn't have found your brain tumor. By the way, Reagan is a wonderful person. She has an amazing spirit. What else do you want to talk about?"

"Well, for the last couple of weeks, every

spirit I have met keeps repeating the message of the sermon, that we are all one and should love one another. Even if I accept that you don't make bad people, some are real . . . what's the term? Oh yeah, motherf—." Still smiling, Rose raised her hand, stopping me cold, and I swallowed the rest. "You know what I mean! How do you welcome with open arms people who do things that are pure evil? To use a medical analogy, aren't *they* a cancer that needs to be removed?"

"So, you're better than they are?"

"Sure. I mean, I think so. How do you forgive and accept people who commit heinous acts?"

"Let's be honest with each other. You were supposed to be at a 9:00 meeting in the twin towers on 9/11, weren't you?"

I nodded.

"That meeting was cancelled because one of the people who was also supposed to be there had a board meeting at church on

Monday, so he couldn't be in New York for a Tuesday-morning meeting. That meeting was changed to the following week. You were living in Chicago at the time and you took Reagan to a Cubs game, instead of flying to New York. When you passed O'Hare, you noticed a 747 seemingly hanging in the air as it was landing and you asked Reagan if she could imagine a plane like that hitting a building. That was another example of how close the living world is connected with the next. You saw what was going to happen, but you didn't understand the message.

"You've felt guilty ever since, wondering why those people died and you didn't. Your friend whose church meeting caused your meeting in New York to be rescheduled told you God has a purpose for you. You told him you disagreed. You said that meant God didn't have a purpose for all who died. Did I get all that right?"

I again nodded and managed a weak, "Yes. That's right."

"Well, honey, that's not the way it works. Like I said, God doesn't reward or punish people, and God doesn't pull the strings. People make decisions, *but* those decisions have consequences, some of which appear to be good, and some that don't."

"What do you mean they 'appear' to be good or bad?"

Rose grinned. "Because the consequences of many of the things that happen to people can only be seen by looking back on them. On the other hand, God sees everything in real time."

"So, you're telling me there was something good about all those people dying on 9/11? And if you, or God, or whatever, has a hands-off policy, why the hell should we pray?"

"Try to not get testy," Rose scolded with a smile. "I didn't say the deaths on 9/11 were a good thing. They just happened. But, God sent spirits, angels if you will, to hold each person's hand and heart as they came home. God did the same for Andy and everyone else who enters Heaven."

"Even the bastards who flew the planes into the towers?"

"Yes, even the men who flew the planes."

"Why?"

Rose said, "I'm sorry you're not getting this. No one earns his or her way into Heaven. People enter Heaven by God's grace. God loves you, darlin', but no more than the men who flew the planes into the towers that morning. God's angels were with them too. And, when the fog was lifted, they saw what they had done and fell to their knees in horror because they understood that all of God's creatures are one. What is done to one is done to all. God loves all of Creation, and thrills at your happiness and cries when you are sad.

"Prayer is a special time for God because it means you are reaching out to have a talk. Nothing makes God happier. But, asking something in prayer doesn't mean God will simply grant your wishes like a genie. Still, God listens and looks for ways to help you find a pathway to reaching your goals, as long as those goals aren't designed to harm or take advantage of someone else.

"Have you ever had a problem you were trying to solve when an idea popped into your head? An idea that showed you a way forward? Do you honestly think that idea simply came to you? Remember, no coincidences. Next question?"

I saw Trudy was licking Andy's hand. "Well, this may sound silly, but I've always wondered why dogs love us. Why our pets love us. I mean, I understand why we love them. They are cuddly and forgiving. But, why do they care for us? We're not dogs." I added in jest, "Well, Pug sort of is. Seriously, why does Trudy love us? We're a different species."

"Because, honey, you may look different, but you were all created in the image of God, even Trudy. She understands that, maybe better than you do. So, who's smarter?"

"Ouch." I looked at Rose. "Okay, I think I understand, but I'm not sure I can do this. I mean, I don't try to be a jerk. I actually try to be a nice guy. I'm not very good at it, but I hear you. I'll keep trying to remember we are all one and I should love others without judging them."

Rose patted my hand. "That's good, sugar. And, you won't be alone. God will be here to help you and to talk whenever you want. Now, I want you to do two things for me."

"What's that?"

"I want you to think about all the conversations you have had over the last couple of weeks and what you want to do with them."

I was again aware of my monitor beeping in the background.

"Okay. What else?"

"Open your eyes."

The beeping sound was louder. My eyes fluttered open. As my vision cleared, I saw Carol's big brown eyes brimming with tears. She started covering my face with kisses. I managed to say, "I thought you were Trudy."

She pulled her head back, laughing. "What? Thanks a lot. You thought I was the dog?"

"It's a long story."

"So is the one about why you're here. I'll tell you all about it, but how are you feeling?"

"I'm okay. My head hurt before Rose took the pain away."

From somewhere off to my right, I heard, "I'm so glad you're awake, sweetheart, and that you're feeling better."

"Rose!"

"Well, darlin', I'm impressed you know my name."

"Of course I know you. You're a godsend."

Carol said, "We've all been so worried about you. The kids have been here and so have our neighbors. Someone named Sally, who helps out here at the hospital with very sick kids, said she had met you at Cuppa, and she has been here almost every day to check on you. Even Barry from the salt spa has been here. I knew you went that one time, but I didn't know you had been going regularly."

"Yeah, well, there's a lot to talk about. But later. I'm too tired now. Maybe just hold my hand?"

Carol said, "Forever."

EPILOGUE

After I finally left the hospital and was home, I shared my story with Carol and showed her my notes. She listened and asked questions, but didn't criticize me or make fun of me, even though it all sounds so incredible. Since I actually have notes, there is no question that I thought these things were really happening to me.

Still, there is the brain tumor. It's entirely possible that pressure on my brain was simply making me believe all this was real.

That wouldn't account for my encounter with Rose before I awoke in the hospital, but it's possible that was just a fog caused by the meds I was on.

The safe thing for my sanity, and to avoid the inevitable fallout of someone discovering this is my story, would be to forget it. It never happened. Life will go on happily. But, there's a voice inside of me saying it is important to share my story with others.

My friend who told me long ago that perhaps God has a purpose for me may have been right, after all. Maybe God doesn't decide our fate, but He still knows what will happen.

So, with Carol's blessing, I decided to push back against my fear and share with you what happened to me. I figured if I didn't, I wouldn't be worth my salt . . . God help me if I made the wrong choice.

BOOK CLUB DISCUSSION

1. In his Prologue, Tom worries about how people are going to receive his story. How would you react if someone told you these things actually happened to him/her?

2. Tom uses his notes with Carol and with us to support the story of his journey. Is it easier for you to believe his story was a result of his brain tumor rather than a real interaction with God? Explain why.

3. What are Tom's character flaws? How about his strengths?

4. Tom is embarrassed as he is forced to examine things he has said and done that are hurtful to others. Share something you have done this week…today, that is hurtful to others.

5. Who was your favorite messenger? Why.

6. Pug tells us that the universe is vast and that God speaks to us regularly in ways we can understand. What do you think about Pug's message?

7. What are the implications of the concept that we are all one, created in God's image?

8. How do the salt messages relate to things that are happening in our world today? If

we truly listened to them, how would it help us make a difference?

9. Sally said, "God didn't create any bad people. People sometimes do bad things." How do you feel about that?

10. Rose said God doesn't "pull the strings" and let bad things happen to people, but sends angels to help us when we need them. She said God didn't give Reagan cancer, but He used that to have a personal relationship with both Reagan and Tom. How do her comments fit with your beliefs?

ACKNOWLEDGMENTS

I didn't write this story, it wrote itself. I was just the one who pushed the keys on my laptop in response to a very unusual confluence of events. Divine inspiration? Perhaps so. God works in mysterious ways. I am grateful for my many blessings.

ABOUT THE AUTHOR

Rick Strater was born in Miami, Florida, to creative parents who were both talented artists. He says that his brother inherited all of the artistic skills.

The family moved to the Midwest when Rick was young, but he insists his birthplace resulted in what he swears is a congenital weakness against the cold weather he detests.

Still, he acknowledges moving north was

necessary for him to meet the love of his life, Natalie, when they were cast as Lancelot and Guinevere in *Camelot*. When he sang "If Ever I Would Leave You" to her, he meant it.

Balancing his right-brained interest in music and writing with his analytical side, he studied business at Indiana University, where he received a bachelor's degree and an MBA before embarking on a successful career in key leadership roles with several large Fortune 500 companies and becoming a cofounder of a tech firm.

Throughout his career, Rick has believed in the power of disruptive thinking in order to drive ever-improving results. He brings this focus on thinking differently to his writing. *Existential Thread*, his first novel, is a superb example of how he creatively captures both the potential benefits and threats represented by advanced 3-D printing and artificial intelligence and forces the reader to begin to seriously consider how we should prepare for both.

After living for decades in the Midwest and on the East Coast, where they raised their four amazing children, Rick finally convinced Natalie that it was time to escape cold weather and high taxes. He wanted to live on the ocean and Natalie wanted to live on a lake where she could have four seasons, so they "compromised" . . . They live on a lake in northern Georgia, and Rick, who is very happy, heads to the ocean every chance he gets.

ALSO BY RICK STRATER